How can you tell if your babysitter is a vampire?

I walked into the front hall and started rummaging around. Glaring, Vincent followed me in. He stood right behind me—and right in front of the mirror. . . .

"You will go back upstairs now." It was not a question. "I will take you."

"Oh, no, that's okay," I said quickly. "I can get up there myself."

I darted a look over at the mirror.

I don't remember what I said next. Somehow I babbled my way up the stairs and back into my room without screaming. And I'm sure Vincent never noticed what I had noticed.

My brother was right. Vincent had no reflection at all.

My Babysitter
Is a Vampire

by
Ann Hodgman

Illustrated by
John Pierard

A GLC Book

A MINSTREL® BOOK

PUBLISHED BY POCKET BOOKS

New York   London   Toronto   Sydney   Tokyo   Singapore

For Laura, who loves babysitters;
for John, who loves dinosaurs;
and for Jean Chapin, who knows how
to run a children's library.

A MINSTREL PAPERBACK *ORIGINAL*

A Minstrel Book published by
POCKET BOOKS, a division of Simon & Schuster Inc.
1230 Avenue of the Americas, New York, NY 10020

Special thanks to Ruth Ashby and Pat MacDonald.

Cover painting by Jeffrey Lindberg
Illustrations by John Pierard
Book Design by Paula Keller
Typesetting by Jackson Typesetters
Developed by Byron Preiss and Daniel Weiss
Senior Editor: Sarah Feldman
Assistant Editor: Kathy Huck

ISBN: 0-671-64751-2

First Minstrel Books printing July 1991
10 9 8 7 6 5 4 3 2 1

A MINSTREL BOOK and colophon are registered trademarks of Simon & Schuster Inc.

Printed in the U.S.A.

PROLOGUE

"Goodbye! Goodbye!" called my little brother Trevor.

"Come back! Come back!" I called even louder.

From the deck of the ferry that was pulling away from the island, our babysitter, Libby Levin, waved happily back at Trevor and me. "Have a great summer, guys!" she yelled, tucking a lock of blond hair behind her ear.

"We can't!" I yelled back. "Not without you!"

Libby's smile flickered for a second, but she readjusted it. "Oh, you'll do great! You won't even know I'm—"

Just then the ferry horn blared out three times. As usual, the blast was so loud that it practically knocked us over. And it cut off whatever else Libby had been about to say. By the time the noise had faded, the ferry was too far away for Trevor and me to hear her anymore. All we could see was her hand fluttering a last goodbye in the fog.

Around us, the people who had just gotten off the ferry were gathering together their suitcases and backpacks and bikes. Like people everywhere about to start vacations, they all seemed to be in terrible moods. "Because my hands are full, Tracy, that's why," I heard one mother snap at her little girl. "You had to bring along your gerbils. *You* carry them."

A cold, gray fog was swirling thick around the dock now. It made the departing ferry look like some kind of ghost ship about to plunge off into the mists at the edge of the world.

I shivered. "Looks haunted," I muttered. "Let's go home, Trevor."

Trevor slipped his damp little hand into mine, and we turned to leave the dock. Suddenly I stopped. I had just caught sight of someone— someone very strange.

It—he, I mean—was a tall, pale boy moving slowly through the crowd. He had probably just gotten off the ferry, but I hadn't noticed him before. Now I wondered how I could have missed him.

For one thing, he really *was* pale. Not white like a sheet of paper, but not the color of any person I had ever seen before, either. His skin was a sickly grayish white, except for his lips, which were a dull maroon. He was dressed entirely in black—black pants, black shirt, and

2

heavy black shoes. His eyes were black, too, and staring vacantly straight ahead. He seemed to be about sixteen, but it was hard to tell for sure. Among the rumpled, shorts-wearing crowd on the dock, he looked as out of place as a toadstool in a bunch of daisies.

And then he stopped moving, bent down, and hoisted something onto his shoulder. Something terribly heavy—so heavy he immediately began staggering under its weight.

It looked exactly like a coffin.

Oh, stop, I scoffed at myself. *It's just his suitcase.*

Sure, I couldn't help saying back to myself. *A black wooden suitcase that's six feet long.*

As I stood watching, the boy shouldered his way through the crowd. In a couple of minutes he disappeared from sight.

"What are you looking at, Meg?" asked Trevor in a small voice.

"Oh, just some weird New Yorker. I'm sure we'll never see him again. Let's get going, Trev. The fog's really coming in now."

My brother wasn't paying any attention to me. He had twisted around to stare at the ferry. "I wish Libby hadn't left," he finally said. "Who do you think Mom and Dad will find to babysit for us now?"

I sighed. "I'm sure they'll manage to scrape

someone off the beach—I mean, I'm sure they'll find someone nice. You just wait and see."

I might have cheered Trevor up, but I hadn't convinced myself at all. As we trudged lonesomely home through the now cold, thick fog, I couldn't shake the feeling that something awful was lying in wait for us that summer.

CHAPTER ONE

None of this would have happened if Libby hadn't decided she liked horses better than Trevor and me.

"Me" is Meg Swain. Or should that be " 'me' *am* Meg Swain?" Anyway, *I'm* Meg Swain. I'm eleven years old, and I'm going into the sixth grade. My brother, Trevor, is six. And Libby Levin, our babysitter, is sixteen.

Except that on the afternoon the ferry pulled away into the fog, Libby had just stopped being our babysitter. She was heading for a horseback-riding camp on the mainland and leaving Trevor and me all alone in the clutches of our parents.

No, that's not fair of me. Mom and Dad aren't really the kind of parents who *have* clutches that you get left in. They're nice enough. It's just that they're very—well, I'll fill you in on my parents later. The point is that Libby had taken care of Trevor and me every summer for the past six years—ever since we started spending our sum-

6

mers on Moose Island, where Libby's family lives year-round. She was practically a member of *our* family. And now that she was about to leave, none of us could imagine what we would do without her.

Moose Island is off the southern coast of Maine, but it's so tiny you may have never heard of it. It's more like a giant rock with a town around the edges and some pine trees in the middle, my friend Jack says. I guess Moose Rock wouldn't have sounded too good—but actually, the Moose part of the name doesn't make much sense, either. The whole middle of the island is a state forest, but I don't know anyone who's ever seen a single moose there. What we mostly have are field mice and quail and rabbits and bats. But Bat Rock would have been an even *worse* name. So it's been Moose Island forever, and we feel as though we've been coming here forever.

We haven't, though. Just six years, as I said. My dad is a screenwriter. We first came to Moose Island when he wanted a quiet place to spend the summer while he worked on a movie project. "I'm not going *near* a phone," he kept telling everyone firmly. So we rented an old, rambling house in the woods with a path to the beach, and we all fell in love with the place—even though it turned out that Moose Island had telephones just like anywhere else, and Dad got just as many calls as ever. Now he has a little office in town, without a phone, and he comes home to our beach house at the end of the day.

My dad wasn't going to be home much this summer at all. He had a big project due at the end of August, and I could tell it was all he was thinking about. Even during our first few days on the island, Dad brought a notebook along to the beach, in case he was seized by sudden inspiration.

"How can you stand using a pen that has sand all over the point?" I asked him once.

"Honey, I'm too busy to let things like that bother me," he answered proudly.

He always broke down and decided to go swimming, instead of sitting on the sand waiting for inspiration. *Then* he always got cranky because he hadn't done any work. Sometimes I wished he'd just stayed home at our real house in Delaware and let the rest of us go on vacation by ourselves.

On the other hand, my mother wasn't going to have much of a vacation either. Mom's in medical school, and she was supposed to work in Moose Island's summer medical center for July and August. She'd be working a lot of night shifts, since it was just her and one other doctor.

So that's my parents. Those are their jobs, any-way. (The other stuff about them isn't interesting enough for you to hear about.) And their being so busy was the reason that Trevor and I needed a babysitter again. I was sure I was the only eleven-year-old on the whole island who still had a baby-sitter instead of being a babysitter herself.

"So tell your parents you can take care of Trevor!" my friend Jack Cornell said. "*I'll* tell them for you!"

"Thanks, Jack, but they won't listen to you any more than they will to me." I took a doleful swig of orange juice. "They say that I can stay home alone, but I'm not old enough to take care of Trevor alone. It's a little insulting, if you think about it."

Mom had been home when Trevor and I got back from seeing Libby off. So Trevor was with her now, and I was over at Jack's house—com-plaining, mostly.

I have lots of friends on Moose Island, but Jack is my best friend there. We became friends when we were little and never outgrew each other. He's going into seventh grade, and his family lives on the island year-round just like Libby's. The Cor-nells' house is a little bit down the beach from ours.

9

Jack's a great person to complain to because he gets so mad. He has way more of a temper than I do—way more of almost every emotion, actually. "Except scaredy-catness," he once told me. "You're a total coward, Meg." I was too much of a coward to deny it.

Now, as he took a fierce bite of his apple (his mother is big on fruit snacks), Jack looked absolutely furious.

"I can't *stand* that your parents are being so stupid!" he said. "It's—it's just *supremely* unfair!" He took another bite of apple. "I mean, look at me! I've—"

"Gross! Don't talk with your mouth full!" I interrupted.

"Sorry." Jack swallowed vigorously. "I mean, look at me!" he repeated more clearly. "I've been on my own since I was *eight years old*! My parents *trust* me!"

"Yeah, but your mom doesn't work," I reminded him glumly. "She's home all the time." She was downstairs in the kitchen right then, in fact. That was why we were having apples and orange juice, instead of the brownies we had seen sitting on the counter.

"Well, I know she's *home*, but she doesn't *guard* me every second the way your parents do. She lets me do anything I want!"

That was pretty much true. Of course, it helps that Jack rarely does anything wrong. He's very responsible—for a seventh grader. But you don't point that kind of thing out when someone's getting angry on your behalf.

"I guess my parents are more protective," I said wearily. "Anyway, I don't think Mom and Dad are going to bend on this one. I'd better go home, Jack. It's almost suppertime."

"Call me if you get them to change their minds," said Jack. "Tell them *I'll* help babysit, if that will make them feel better."

It didn't.

"Honey, you can't be serious! Why, Jack blew up a house once!" my mother protested when I got home and suggested Jack's plan to her.

"A *treehouse*, Mom! And he didn't blow it up—he burned it down!" That was one of the few times Jack *hadn't* been very responsible. "Besides, it was just part of a science experiment!"

"The fact that Jack is a friend of yours makes me even more sure that you need a babysitter," my mother said swiftly. She's good at seizing an opportunity. "If Jack ever comes to visit, the sitter can keep an eye on him, too."

I tried a different tack. "Libby started babysitting for us when she was ten!"

But Mom responded with my all-time least-favorite grownup answer. "Libby is Libby. You are you," she said. "Now, let's drop the subject, Meg. You and Trevor are not spending the summer alone."

For the first few days after Libby left, though, it looked as though we weren't going to have any choice. Mom dug up quite a collection of potential babysitters—but they were all total duds.

First we tried Brandie Delton. Or rather, we never got the chance to try her, because she never showed up. So Mom and Dad had to fire someone they never even met.

Then came Josie Yurman. She showed up right on time, but the second my parents were out the door, she headed straight for the kitchen phone and didn't hang up for three hours. Unfortunately for Josie, Mom tried to call home fifteen times during those three hours. (She had forgotten to leave Josie her number at the center.) After call number fifteen, she drove home and fired Josie on the spot.

After Josie came Melissa Gittes, who ate an entire cheesecake that Mom had been saving for company. Then Mom found Bridget Camden.

Bridget was really nice. I could tell right away that we'd be good friends. After all, she was only a year younger than I was.

"You see!" I said triumphantly after my mother

had taken Bridget back home. "If she's old enough to babysit, why aren't I?"

"She's *not* old enough," my mother informed me curtly. "And neither are you. So let's drop the subject for now, okay?"

The next day Mom brought up the subject again herself.

It was during supper when she made the announcement. Dad was working late, and Mom got home so late herself that we all had to rush around to get dinner ready. I could see that she was bursting with some kind of news, but she didn't tell us what it was until we'd all been served.

"I just found the *perfect* babysitter at the medical center!" she crowed. "You guys are going to be so happy!"

Trevor and I, who had both been fishing the mushrooms out of our leftover stew, looked up at her warily.

"What's her name?" I asked after a second.

"*His* name, honey. His name is Vincent. Vincent Graver. He's sixteen years old, and he seems to be free all summer. He works at the blood bank, but it's just a part-time job so he can make his own hours."

"Hey, a boy for once!" said Trevor enthusiastically. "That's neat, Mom!"

Mom smiled at him. "I thought you'd like it."

"What's Vincent like?" I asked cautiously. Being a boy and working at the blood bank didn't seem like much of a recommendation.

"Oh, he's very polite and charming. And very accommodating. He doesn't care how late Dad and I stay out. He even offered to babysit free of charge, but of course I couldn't let him do that. And he said he'd come over tomorrow morning so you can meet him. If you like him and he likes you, he can start here the next day!"

I forgot to mention my cat, didn't I?

I sort of hate funny names for cats, but Pooch deserves his. He's a big, fat, jowly old tiger cat who's just as friendly as a dog—the kind of dog that people joke would invite a burglar into the house. Pooch even takes walks with us. (He always gets too tired to finish, though, because he's such a tub. After a few minutes, he collapses on the side of the road and Mom or Dad has to pick him up.) He runs up to meet us when we come home, and he starts meowing like crazy whenever he sees someone coming to the door. There's no one that cat doesn't like.

That's why Pooch's behavior when he first saw Vincent Graver seemed so strange to me.

When the doorbell rang, Pooch thudded down the stairs, skidded through the front hall, and ran smack into the door just as it was opening.

That was normal. What was *ab*normal was the way Pooch behaved when he saw who was at the door. He let out a startled little yelp—there was no other word for it. Then he streaked across the floor, and dashed under the sofa in the living room. (Of course, he could only get halfway under because he was so fat.)

I saw this from the landing, but I couldn't see who was at the door. "What's the matter with you, Pooch?" I called, laughing. I started down the rest of the stairs. "Why are you so shy all of a—"

Then the door swung open, and Vincent walked in, a little curl of fog swirling in with him.

I froze on the stairs, one foot in midstep.

He wasn't carrying a coffin this time. But the boy staring up at me was the same one I had noticed on the dock the day Libby left.

"Hello," he said in a deep, emotionless voice. "I am Vincent Graver."

He licked his dark red lips.

"And you, I suppose, are little Meg."

CHAPTER TWO

Suddenly I realized that my foot was still hanging in midair. I lowered it slowly to the next step, still staring at Vincent.

"Y-yes, I'm Meg," I finally managed to say. Then I raised my voice and croaked out, "Mom! Vincent's here!"

It sounds silly, I know, but I just didn't want to be alone in the room with him. It was ten o'clock in the morning, my mother was in the house with me, and I could hear birds chirping away in the woods. But I felt as though Vincent had somehow brought the middle of the night right into our front hall. The very air around him seemed colder than that in the rest of the house.

My mother didn't seem to notice, though. She walked into the living room just in time to see Vincent bowing and holding out his hand for me to shake.

What could I do? I shook it.

It was like shaking a rubber glove filled with crushed ice.

"Oh, hello, Vincent," my mother was saying cheerfully. "I'm glad to see you again."

"And I to see *you*," Vincent replied. Again came the little bow. I was amazed to see that my mother looked impressed.

"Let me show you the house," Mom went on. "I've got to leave for work in a few minutes, but there's time for you to—"

"Hey, Mom!" interrupted Trevor, racing down the stairs. "Where's my dinosaur T-shirt? I need it for— Oh, hi!" he said when he saw that there was someone else in the room.

I love my brother, but he's not the most *observant* person in the world. All he's really interested in right now is dinosaurs. I don't think he noticed anything weird about Vincent.

"You are Trevor," said Vincent calmly. "I am pleased to make your acquaintance." Once again he bowed and held out that cold, bloodless hand.

"Trevvie, what do we do when someone holds out a hand?" my mother asked automatically. "We *shake* it." She pushed my brother forward and gave Vincent an apologetic smile. "We're just starting to get around to manners," she said.

For the fourth time Vincent bowed. "A fine

thing to learn, young man," he said to Trevor. And he stretched his mouth in what looked more like a muscle spasm than a smile.

I bit back a gasp. Every one of Vincent's gleaming teeth ended in a point.

"Oh, Meg, for heaven's sake," groaned my father during supper that night. "We don't pick babysitters for their looks!"

"But Dad, Vincent has *pointed teeth*!" I protested. "That's not *normal* bad looks!"

"Maybe he filed them into points," Dad suggested. "Teenagers do that kind of thing sometimes. It's not my favorite sight, I'll admit, but if Vincent likes it, that's all that matters. Don't you ever file *your* teeth, though," he added hastily.

"I don't want to. But Vincent might *influence* me to, if you make me spend the whole summer with him. You know—peer pressure."

Suddenly, my mother dropped her fork with a clatter. She looked tired and upset.

"Honey, I wish you'd stop talking this way," she said. "Daddy and I are very busy. We're working *extremely* hard to make sure that you and Trevor are being taken care of. If you're really afraid of Vincent, then say so and we'll find someone else. But if you're just trying to make us feel bad about having to work so much this summer, then please cut it out. We feel bad enough already."

"What do *you* think about all this, Trevor?" my father interjected. "Do you like Vincent or not?"

Trevor hadn't been paying much attention to the conversation. I think he had been purposely tuning it out—he hates to hear people fighting. He was busy lining up his toy dinosaurs around the rim of his plate. (He's allowed to bring them to the table as long as he doesn't feed them.)

He looked up, startled, at Dad's question. "He's okay, I guess," he said slowly. "I don't like his teeth, but I did want to have a boy babysitter. And now I have one, right?" He bent his head toward his dinosaurs again.

Some ally you are, I thought. "But Trevor, don't you think it's creepy the way he—"

"Now, that's definitely enough," said my mother sharply. "You are *not* to put ideas into your brother's head, Meg."

Well, there wasn't much I could say. I didn't want to cause trouble. And I didn't have anything concrete against Vincent, not really. Nothing, except his pallor and his icy-cold skin and his pointed teeth and his black clothes and the coffin he carried around with him. None of it was anything a *parent* would take seriously.

Besides, I tried to reassure myself, I wouldn't

have to be home that much anyway. Vincent was actually Trevor's babysitter, not mine. And Trevor really was happy about having a boy babysitter for once—as long as I was careful not to scare him from now on.

So by the end of the meal, it was settled. I would stop complaining, and Vincent would start babysitting. Mom and Dad had to go to a party the next night, and Vincent would sit for the first time then. He was due at seven o'clock.

That left me twenty-four Vincent-free hours to enjoy. Plus ten minutes, I figured. Even Libby had never shown up exactly on time.

Unfortunately, Vincent *did* show up exactly on time. The battered old grandfather clock in our front hall was just starting to chime seven when I heard the doorbell ring.

This time Pooch didn't run to the door. He raced under the sofa without even waiting to see who was there.

"Your cat does not like guests, I see," was the first thing Vincent said, as he stepped inside and saw Pooch's back half.

He doesn't like you, anyway, I wanted to answer. But I didn't. I had made up my mind to get along with Vincent. I just giggled nervously and wished Mom and Dad would come downstairs to take the burden of the conversation off me. (Since they always figure every babysitter will be late, they never start getting ready to go out until the last minute.)

"Where's your car?" I asked, peering outside. "Or did someone drop you off?" I hadn't heard a car outside, come to think of it, but I knew Vincent couldn't have walked. I know every family that lives within walking distance of our house.

"I rode my bicycle," answered Vincent.

"Where's your bicycle, then?" I heard myself asking idiotically. Why was I trying to make conversation out of such a stupid topic?

Vincent frowned slightly. "My bicycle is concealed in the woods," he answered. There was a shade of reproof in his voice. "It is a high-quality model. I fear thieves."

It is a high-quality model. I fear thieves. Vincent didn't have an accent, but he sounded as though he had learned to speak English from a book.

My brother came scuffling into the room before I could ask any more stupid questions about Vincent's modes of transportation. He was already in his pajamas—the kind with feet. Trevor is always afraid someone's going to try to tickle his feet while he's sleeping. It's one of the many, many things that makes him wake up a lot during the night.

"Hi, Vincent," he said cheerfully.

21

"Good evening, Trevor."

"Want to see my dinosaur collection?" Trevor asked. "I have six *Tyrannosauruses* and eight *Dimetrodons* and four *Plesiosaurs* and—"

"Trevor, I would very much appreciate seeing your dinosaur collection," Vincent answered in a deep, hollow voice. "Where have you concealed it?"

"Concealed it?" Trevor looked puzzled. "It's over here in this box! Come on, I'll show you."

The two of them were halfway across the room when my parents came rushing down from their bedroom in their usual preparty bustle. Mom was trying to fasten her earrings. I could tell she was secretly trying to hike up her slip at the same time.

"Hi, kids," she said distractedly, checking her reflection in the mirror in the front hallway. "Hi, Vincent. Okay, guys. We're off. The number's by the phone. We won't be back too late, Vincent— no later than midnight, I hope."

"I do not care about the lateness of the hour," said Vincent. "In fact, I prefer a late evening."

My father stared at him quizzically for an instant. *Come on, Dad! Notice how weird he is!* I screamed at him telepathically. But he didn't seem to get my message. "Oh. Well, that's good!"

he said. "See you later, kids." He blew kisses to Trevor and me.

"You guys can order a pizza for dinner," said my mother, giving one last furtive tug at her slip. "And, Vincent, don't worry if Trevor wakes up a couple of times. He's a very light sleeper. And help yourself to anything in the fridge that you want."

"I do not care for between-meal snacks," said Vincent.

"That's a nice change from the usual sitter," Dad said cheerfully to Mom as he reached for the keys hanging by the door. "What was the name of that cheesecake-scarfer we tried out? If we had hired *her*, she probably would have eaten the floor tiles by now. Anyway, so long, kids. Have a great evening!"

He and Mom closed the front door. Then I heard them start the car—and my brother and I were alone with Vincent.

I wanted to be a good sport. I really did. But somehow I just couldn't believe we were going to have a great evening.

CHAPTER THREE

There were a few seconds of silence after we heard the car drive away. Then Trevor looked trustingly up at Vincent.

"We were going to play with my dinosaurs," he reminded him.

"So we were," agreed Vincent in his heavy, slow way. "Let me see your dinosaurs, Trevor."

Trevor has about two hundred of them. (They had a whole suitcase to themselves on the trip here.) He sat down happily on the living room rug and dumped out the box.

Plastic dinosaurs of all colors and sizes skittered across the floor. Trevor rooted around in the pile for a second, then picked up an orange one.

"Here's *Tyrannosaurus rex*," he said. "He's my favorite."

"Ah, yes." Vincent nodded. "A meat-eater."

"And here's *Allosaurus*. He's my second-favorite. No, my third-favorite. No, my second."

"Another meat-eater," said Vincent approvingly. He picked up *Allosaurus* and studied him for a second. "See his sharp, gleaming teeth. Perhaps he is preparing to bite someone."

"And this—who's this? Oh. *Deinonychus*."

"Yessss," said Vincent. His voice sounded almost like a hiss. "With his savage claws, he rips and tears his helpless prey into bloody—"

Suddenly I felt that Vincent was enjoying this conversation a little too much. "And what's this one, Trevor?" I asked quickly, grabbing the dinosaur closest to me.

"*Ankylosaurus*," my brother answered. "He really *is* my third-favorite."

"A plant-eater, merely," Vincent said scornfully. "I greatly prefer the meat-eaters. They must lie in wait for their prey, hoping to—"

"You know, I wouldn't mind some food myself!" I said, interrupting again. I didn't want to give Vincent the chance to tell us anything more about prey. "Pizza, that is. How about ordering our pizza now?"

"Yeah!" said Trevor. "Get it with extra cheese, okay? And no green peppers or green olives. Nothing green."

"What about you, Vincent?" I asked politely. "Do you have any—uh—pizza wishes?"

"As I told your mother, I do not care about pizza," said Vincent. He sounded a little irritated, but I couldn't imagine why.

Moose Island has one tiny, little pizza place that delivers. They're always mobbed. When I placed our order, they told me that it would take forty-five minutes for the pizza to get there.

Forty-five minutes! I *dare* you to sit through forty-five minutes with someone like Vincent!

For one thing, he was turning out to be a terrible conversationalist.

"Are you having a good time working at the blood bank?" I asked.

"It satisfies my needs," was all Vincent answered.

"What—um—what do you do in your spare time?"

"I rest." And he gave an eerie laugh. I've never seen anything especially funny about resting, myself, but of course I'm not Vincent.

Then there was the way he kept staring at Trevor and me. It made me really nervous. For some reason, it reminded me of the way a crocodile I had once seen on one of those TV nature shows had watched a baby bird hopping nearby.

"What's the matter?" I finally asked Vincent. "Do I have something on my nose?"

27

"Nothing is the matter. I am hungry, merely."

"Well, the pizza's on its way," I reminded him uneasily.

Vincent did not reply. I could hear the wind whistling through the trees outside and, far down on the beach, the breakers crashing against the shore. It sounded as though we were going to have a storm that night.

A mouse scuttled through one of the walls behind us. The sound suddenly reminded me of Pooch, who was still cowering halfway under the sofa. I crawled over to him. "Poochie, don't you want to come out now?" I coaxed. I took hold of his plump sides and tried to ease him out a little. But I could tell he was digging his claws into the floor.

"Your cat is an excessively nervous animal," observed Vincent. "He is foolish to be so frightened of strangers."

"Pooch isn't foolish!" I answered tartly. "He's just—"

Suddenly there was a knock on the door.

"Yay!" said Trevor happily, looking up from his dinosaurs at last. "The pizza's here!"

It was a good one, too—thick and crusty, with a bubbling pool of cheese on top. Vincent didn't want any. He just sat silently on the floor with us while we ate it. And he didn't sit all that close, either.

"Aren't you hungry anymore?" I asked him. "This is the best pizza on the island, you know."

Vincent shook his head, wincing. "I cannot stand all that vile garlic," he said.

"What is barlic?" asked Trevor with interest. "Do I like barlic, Meg?"

"*Garlic*, not barlic. And no, you don't like it," I told him. "But you do like this pizza because there's no barlic—I mean garlic—in it."

"Then have some, Vincent!" Trevor held a dripping slice right up to Vincent's mouth. "It's really good!"

But Vincent scrambled out of the way and jumped to his feet. "*I said no!*" he thundered, his face chalk-white. "Keep that stinking mess away from me!"

Startled, Trevor stared up at him for a second. "Okay," Trevor said cheerfully. "I guess there must be some barlic in it after all."

I guess there must have been. And I guess there must have been some garlic in the airwaves when we watched TV after our pizza. Because when a commercial for Aunt Rosie's Extra-Garlic Garlic Bread came on, Vincent started getting even paler. He took his eyes off the set and stared determinedly at the wall. And when the commercial started to describe the bread's wonderful smell, Vincent clapped his hand over his mouth and bolted from the room.

"What's the matter with him?" Trevor was staring wide-eyed at me.

"I have no idea, Trevvie. I have absolutely no idea."

After a couple of minutes Vincent marched back in.

"Feeling better?" I asked him sweetly.

Vincent didn't answer. He just marched over and switched off the television. "Bedtime," he announced abruptly.

"Hey, wait!" I protested. "It's way too early! We're not supposed to go to bed until—"

"Bedtime," Vincent repeated. *Now.*

I was about to argue more when I suddenly noticed something I hadn't seen before. Vincent's fingernails were pointed, too. I mean, most peoples' fingernails are tapered a little, but Vincent's were *pointed.* Like a cat's.

You try arguing when a guy who's as white as a corpse and has pointed fingernails is looming over you. "Okay, Vincent," I said. "Anything you say. Come on, Trevor."

Trevor scooped up a handful of dinosaurs and followed me upstairs. "Good night, Vincent," he said cheerfully.

"Good night," Vincent answered. There was a strange light in his eyes. "Sleep well. Very, very, very well."

* * *

But I didn't sleep very, very, very well. Maybe I couldn't fall asleep because it was still too early. I had helped Trevor brush his teeth, read him a story, and tucked him into bed. Then I had gotten ready for bed myself. And now I was *in* bed, feeling as wide awake as if Vincent had sent me to bed at noon.

Well, Vincent had made me come up here, but he couldn't make me fall asleep. I decided to read for a while. I switched on my bedside lamp and reached over the side of the bed for my new pile of library books.

The little library on Moose Island is one of my favorite places. It's in a stone building that overlooks the ocean, and it has books that you never see anywhere else—old, mildewy books about girl detectives in boarding school and girls who tame wild mares and girls who learn to sew so they can support their widowed mothers.

It also has a decent collection of murder mysteries and old ghost stories. And what I picked up from the floor right then was a book called *The Haunting of Windy Harbor.*

Oh, good! I thought, snuggling back against the pillows. I *love* horror stories. I flipped the book to the first page and began to read.

After a few pages, though, I started to feel a little uncomfortable as I read.

Outside, a miserable wind was moaning like

a soul in torment. Branches tapped the window-pane as gently as the bony fingers of skeleton children. Within the house, Kathryne lay in bed, paralyzed with fear. The ghost was back again. She was sure of it. And this time, it was in the house.

The air in the house had gone bone-cold. The clocks had all stopped ticking. And now, slowly and stealthily, someone was creeping up the stairs.

Now it was on the first step. Kathryne heard its bony feet scrabbling on the bare wood. Now it was on the second step. It paused on the landing, as if to gather its thoughts. Now it was at the top of the stairs. And now it was inching slowly, slowly toward her bedroom door. . . .

I slammed the book shut. This was not the kind of thing that was going to waft me off to dreamland! I tossed *The Ghost of Windy Harbor* to the floor and picked up *Betsy in Spite of Herself* instead.

The Betsy books are pretty relaxing, even though Betsy makes such a fool of herself most of the time that you just want to scream at her. After a half an hour of reading about her schemes to get to ride in the red roadster of a boy named Phil, I decided I was tired enough to fall asleep. I switched off the light and lay down flat.

But as I lay there, the ghost of Windy Harbor

began to slither back into my thoughts. I was all alone in our house, after all—or as good as. And we lived near a harbor—a beach, anyway. And I could hear strange sounds . . .

I really could. I'm sure it wasn't my imagination. The wind suddenly started to howl as if it were doing its best to imitate the wind in my ghost book.

You've heard storms before, I told myself. *You're not a chicken about the weather.*

Our beach house is perfectly comfortable, but it *is* a beach house. I mean, it doesn't have a lot of insulation. So if you're upstairs, you can hear what's going on downstairs pretty clearly.

And what I could hear was that someone was really creeping up the stairs.

Well, of course, I said sternly to myself. *It's Vincent. He's coming up to check on everything, just the way a good babysitter should.*

But if that was true, then why was he sneaking up the stairs so—so stealthily?

Because he doesn't want to wake us up, I told myself again. *It's perfectly normal.*

Now the top step—which creaks no matter how lightly you try to walk on it—was creaking. I *know* that wasn't my imagination.

Vincent—if it was Vincent—stopped suddenly. Then the hushed, cautious footsteps began again.

They were creeping toward my door.

And now my doorknob was turning. Gently, gently it was being turned.

The wind screamed outside my window, and suddenly a bolt of lightning crackled through the sky.

Thanks stupid weather. You're doing a lot to calm me down.

Now my door was opening, a fraction of an inch at a time. In a couple of seconds, it would—

I couldn't take it anymore.

I rolled over loudly in bed. "H-hello?" I said groggily, as though I had suddenly woken up. "Who's there?"

"Meg?" called Trevor instantly from down the hall. I told you, he wakes up just like *that.*

The door froze in its tracks—if that's the way you describe it. Then, as slowly and soundlessly as it had opened, it began to shut again.

In a couple of seconds, I heard the stairs creaking again. Whoever it was outside my room was going back down.

"It-it's nothing, Trevor," I called out in as normal a voice as I could manage. "Go back to sleep now."

But what had just happened pretty much wrecked *my* chances for falling asleep. For the next few hours I lay rigidly awake, waiting for

34

my parents to come home. And I have never been happier than when I heard their car pulling up outside.

"Okay, Vincent. Thanks very much," I heard my father saying downstairs. "Sure you don't want a ride home? It's raining pretty hard. I could put your bike in the back of the car."

"I am quite sure, Mr. Swain," said Vincent politely. "I enjoy riding at night. But I appreciate your generous offer."

"Okay, then. Thanks again," said Dad.

"See you soon, I hope!" chirped my mother.

"I look forward to our next meeting with great anticipation," Vincent replied. I was sure he was bowing again.

As soon as the front door closed, I jumped out of bed and tiptoed to my window. I wanted to watch Vincent leaving. I wanted to make *sure* he was leaving.

A sudden flash of lightning lit everything up for a second, and I saw that Vincent was walking straight into the rainswept woods.

To get his bike?

No. He couldn't be getting his bike. He wasn't even using the path—he was just crashing off into the soggy underbrush.

Why? I wondered. There wasn't anything in

that direction except woods. Woods, and a little abandoned shack that hunters had used about fifty years ago . . .

Out of nowhere a bat swooped crazily toward my window—straight toward my face.

Heart pounding, I slammed the window shut. I think I made it across to the bed in one leap. But it was a long, long time before I finally fell asleep.

CHAPTER FOUR

When I woke up the next morning, the storm was over. Sun was pouring into my room, and I could smell Mom's blueberry muffins down in the kitchen. I jumped out of bed and began to get dressed.

As I threw on a T-shirt, I decided I had just been imagining things the night before. I gave *The Haunting of Windy Harbor* a scornful kick. Trust me to get scared by a book that hadn't even been checked out in forty years! As Jack said, I was a total coward. But there was certainly nothing to be scared of on a day like this.

"Good morning, sweetie," Mom greeted me as I bounced into the kitchen. "How'd things go with Vincent last night?"

"Oh, fine," I said.

"Well, that's good, because I've got to cover at the center today. So Vincent's going to be coming over again."

My sunny mood clouded up a bit. It's easy

enough to be a good sport about something when it's behind you. It's a little harder when you've got to crank up the good-sport engine all over again.

But after all, I reminded myself, *I* didn't have to stick around just because Mom was going to be gone. So right after breakfast I called Jack.

"Hi!" I said perkily when he answered. "I wondered if you'd like to get together for a swim. It's a perfect day for it!"

Jack paused. "This is Maine, Meg," he said. "Cold water at the beginning of the summer, remember? *Icy* water—the kind you're always complaining about. We need a few ninety-degree days before the ocean will be swimmable. Your dad's the only one who goes in this early. Besides, it's supposed to turn foggy later this morning."

"I don't remember complaining about the water," I lied. "I love cold water. I inherited it from my dad. It's so—you know—refreshing and everything."

"Okay," said Jack. "What time would you like me to come over?"

"No, what time would you like *me* to come over?"

"You're inviting yourself over here?"

"Thanks! I'd love to!—Hang on a second." I put the phone down. "Mom, what time do you have to go to work?" I asked.

"About eleven-thirty," she answered.

I picked up the phone again. "Jack? Make that a swim *and* lunch. At your house."

So then, of course, I had to pretend I liked swimming in negative-degree water in the fog. But at least I had managed to get out of the house while Vincent was there.

And the night after that, when Mom had to spend a couple of hours at work after supper, my friend Darcy invited me to go to the movies with her. And the day after that—a wet, blowy day— there was a litter pick-up on Main Street, and of course I didn't mind saving the planet in the rain when a creep like Vincent was babysitting at my house. So that took care of the third day.

In fact, I was pretty sure that if I planned things carefully, the only times I'd ever have to see Vincent would be when he was arriving at our house and I was leaving it.

But that was before my talk with Trevor.

Now, all this time I'd been staying away from the house, I'd assumed that Trevor was doing fine. He *liked* Vincent, after all. Trevor always got along with people. When there were things he didn't like about a person, he just tuned them out. I was sure he was happily playing with his dinosaurs and paying no attention to Vincent at all.

But a few days later when I was eating lunch

(a ham and cheese sandwich whose cheese kept falling out) and my parents were outside gardening, Trevor's voice came floating down from upstairs.

"Meg? Could you come up here?"

"Can I finish my sandwich before it gets away from me?" I yelled as a piece of cheese slithered out again.

"Um—no," my brother answered. "It has to be right now."

"Oh, alllll riiiiiight," I groaned. I put down my sandwich and went upstairs to Trevor's room.

When I walked in, I saw that for once Trevor wasn't playing with his dinosaurs. Instead, he was standing in front of the mirror, gazing anxiously at his reflection.

"What's the matter, dude? Are freckles blemishing that perfect complexion?" I asked.

Trevor didn't take his eyes off himself. "People usually have reflections in mirrors, don't they?" he asked carefully.

"Of course they do! They always do! When they're standing in front of mirrors, anyway."

"Vincent doesn't."

"What's that?" I asked, startled.

"Vincent doesn't have one. He doesn't have a reflection."

Trevor's voice was trembling a little. "Don't you think he *ought* to have one?" he asked.

"Wait a minute, Trev." I sat down on the edge of his bed. "Tell me what you're talking about."

Trevor turned to face me. His eyes were round and troubled. "Well, you know how last night Vincent was babysitting and you weren't here?"

One of my friends had had a slumber party, thank heaven. "Yes," I answered.

"Vincent was standing in front of the hall mirror, and his reflection wasn't there." Trevor's voice was quavering a little. "Do you think he could have—lost it?"

I couldn't help smiling. "Oh, Trevor! People don't lose their reflections. The light must have been weird or something."

I leaned forward to rumple his hair, but he jerked out of the way. "Vincent didn't have a reflection," he insisted. "And the light *wasn't* weird, because I saw myself in the mirror behind him." He shivered. "Meg, I was standing behind Vincent. I could see right through him!"

"Honey, that kind of thing just doesn't happen in real life." I made my voice as reassuring as I could. "Did you tell Mommy about it?"

My brother shook his head. "I wanted *you* to tell her for me. Tell her to send him home!"

I paused. Trevor was really unhappy, and even though he drives me crazy sometimes, I don't like to see him upset. But I couldn't see telling Mom something like this, because there was absolutely no way she'd believe it. "Mom, Trevor couldn't see Vincent's reflection in the mirror." What kind of thing was that to tell a mother who was already a little mad at you for being uncooperative? I was afraid that my mother would only think I was trying to make more trouble for her. And I really didn't want to do that.

"Trevor, I don't think either of us should tell Mom about this. Not yet, anyway. There's no sense in making her worry about us when she's so busy. Besides, what's important about Vincent is that he takes such good care of us—not the fact that you didn't see him in the mirror."

Do I get the prize for being Mom-ish, or what?

"And now," I suggested, "let's go play with your dinosaurs."

Trevor's face brightened. "All right!" he said happily, and raced out of the room ahead of me.

I hardly knew what to think about this. I hoped I'd managed to smooth things over. But I was starting to realize that Trevor might think Vincent was just as weird as I thought. I was sure he did the next night, when Mom and Dad both had to go out after supper.

"Guys, could you clear the table?" Mom called down from her bedroom. "I've got to change, and Vincent's going to be here any minute."

Ann Hodgman

Trevor was just finishing his dessert. As I reached over to pick up the dishes next to him, he suddenly grabbed my sleeve.

"You're not going out tonight, too, are you?" he asked pleadingly.

"Well, actually, I am," I admitted reluctantly. "Jack's mom is picking me up so I can go over there and watch a movie on their VCR." We don't have a VCR at the beach house. I complain about it constantly. "She should be here in a couple of—"

"Meg, don't go!" There were tears in my brother's eyes. "Don't leave me alone with him!" Trevor begged. "I don't like him! H-he's yucky! I can't stay with him anymore!" Trevor was really crying now. "Please stay here," he begged for the third time. "I-I'll clear all these dishes myself if you will!"

Now there was a lump in my throat, too. I felt terrible. I hadn't been thinking about Trevor all this time—only about getting away from Vincent. And my poor little brother, who had no way of getting out of the house, had been as creeped-out as I was.

I gave Trevor a quick hug. "Oh, Trev. You don't have to clear all by yourself. I'll go call Jack now and tell him I'm staying here. You finish your cheesecake. And then let's clean up together."

While I dialed Jack's number, I made a quick resolution. I wouldn't leave Trevor alone with Vincent anymore. It was too mean.

And I would solve the mirror mystery that night.

The evening with Vincent was just as weird as before. Vincent still refused to eat anything. He still stared strangely at Trevor and me. He still talked more like a zombie than a real person.

And he still sent us up to bed way too early. This time, though, I didn't fuss about it. I went up obediently, tucked Trevor in, got into my own pajamas, and sat in my room to wait.

From the sounds on the first floor, I could tell that Vincent was watching TV. I waited through the first commercial, until the regular program—whatever it was—had started up again. (You can always tell when a commercial's on because it's about ten thousand times louder than the regular show.) Then I slipped out of my room and began to tiptoe down the stairs.

It was just like my nightmarish time the other night—except that now things were reversed. *I* was the one creeping down the stairs, not the one being crept up on (if you see what I mean). But I felt just as scared doing it as I had felt listening to it the other night. Which is worse, waiting

for something horrible to sneak up on you—or sneaking up on something horrible yourself?

Whichever it is, I was terribly nervous. And when I got a glimpse of the TV screen, I almost fell down the stairs.

A monster that looked like a mound of bloody Shredded Wheat was lurching across some kind of bone-strewn floor with an axe in its hand. As I watched, it prepared to sink the axe into the skull of some kind of greenish monster tied down to a long black table. (Or it could have been an orangeish monster. The color on our TV isn't too good.) The monster's eyes fluttered open, and Mr. Shredded Wheat drew back for a second. Then, with a heartstopping shriek, it raised the axe again, and—

"Heh-heh. Heh-heh. Heh-heh."

Vincent hadn't seen me. He was sitting on the sofa and chortling quietly to himself. You know the way Bert laughs on "Sesame Street"? That's exactly what Vincent sounded like—except that the effect was a little different coming from Vincent.

"They always make so many *mistakes* on these shows!" he said, chuckling to himself. "So many *inaccuracies*! It is quite, quite ridiculous."

Then he reached into his pocket and pulled

something out. I squinted through the bannister to see what it was.

It was a silver flask. As I watched, Vincent unscrewed the top and took a huge, gulping drink.

Who carries soda around in a flask? I wondered like a moron.

"Ahhh." Vincent sighed contentedly. Then he turned back toward the television—and I saw his face.

Vincent's lips were gleaming with some kind of bright red liquid. A thin line of red was trickling down his chin. And the rim of the flask was gleaming red as well.

That time, I did fall down the stairs.

"What are you doing here?" Vincent hissed. He had crossed the room in three strides and was looming over me. "I ordered you to go to sleep half an hour ago!"

"I—I—" I sat up, struggling for breath. "I forgot something!"

"What is it?" The flask was nowhere in sight. Vincent must have stuffed it back into his pocket.

"It's—uh—my diary. I need it. To write in—you know? It's where I put *all* my most special thoughts." I knew I was babbling, but I couldn't stop myself. "Can't get to sleep until I write in my diary!"

"Where is this diary?" Vincent asked severely.

"I—I think it's in the front hall. Where all my new library books are."

And where the mirror was.

I walked into the front hall and started rummaging around. Glaring, Vincent followed me in. He stood right behind me—and right in front of the mirror.

"Wait, it's not with my library books," I chattered. "Maybe it's in the closet, or under these rainboots here. Wow, they're muddy! Do you think it's going to keep being so rainy and foggy all summer?"

"Where is the diary?" Vincent said implacably.

"N-not in here, I guess."

Of course it wasn't. I'd never kept a diary in my life.

I stood up and smiled apologetically at Vincent. "Sorry. I guess I must have left it at school. I mean, at Jack's house."

"You will go back upstairs now." It was not a question. "I will take you."

"Oh, no, that's okay," I said quickly. "I can get up there myself."

I darted a look over at the mirror.

I don't remember what I said next. Somehow I

babbled my way up the stairs and back into my room without screaming. And I'm sure Vincent never noticed what I had noticed.

My brother was right. Vincent had no reflection at all.

CHAPTER FIVE

"He's a vampire," said Jack instantly.

"Oh, come on," I answered.

"Come on yourself! What else could he possibly be? Pointed teeth, dressed in black, drinks blood—"

"We don't *know* that it was blood," I interrupted.

"Drinks blood," Jack repeated firmly. "And has no reflection! Haven't you ever watched horror movies, Meg?"

"Of course I haven't! You know that!"

"Oh, that's right. You're a coward. Well, if you *did* have the guts to watch horror movies, you would know that vampires don't have reflections."

As you can probably tell, I had been filling Jack in on what had happened with Vincent the night before. And as you can also probably tell, Jack had come up with a pretty unbelievable suggestion.

"Those are just movies, Jack," I reminded him.

"The stuff in them isn't necessarily true, you know. *Vampires* aren't even true," I went on. "I mean, they don't exist. You're really kind of— uh—jumping to conclusions." I felt a little smug. I don't often get the chance to act older than Jack.

Jack didn't look as though I'd scored any points. He was staring at me as if *I* was the one jumping to conclusions.

"Let's go on down to the library, then," he said. "We'll just look up vampires and see who's right."

"Do you have any Spiderman books?" asked a little boy in a piercing voice.

The librarian, Mr. Stives, shook his head and raised a warning finger to his lips. Mr. Stives can't stand people making noise in the children's section of the library—as though there's any *point* in having a kids' library and making everyone be quiet!

"Do you have any Spiderman puzzles?" asked the little boy again.

"No, we don't," whispered Mr. Stives.

"Well, don't you have *any* Spiderman stuff?"

Mr. Stives shook his head smilingly. I doubt he had any idea of what the boy was talking about. Mr. Stives is about five hundred years old. He must have forgotten what it's like to be a kid long before movies and TV were invented. Or even comic books.

But he had been able to help us with vampire books. Jack and I were sitting in the library's tiny research area with a pile of them in front of us.

The books were almost as creepy as what they were about. They were even dustier and more mildewed than the regular books at the Moose Island library. Every time I opened one, spiderwebs draped themselves all over my hand. And a couple of times the book covers crumbled off *into* my hands. I hoped I'd be able to slide them back onto the shelves without Mr. Stives seeing what kind of shape they were in.

But they—the books, I mean, not the spiderwebs—were proving Jack's point. Everything they said about vampires described Vincent perfectly.

The white skin. The red lips. The pointed teeth and fingernails. The blood-drinking. (Suddenly, I was sure that the red liquid in Vincent's flask *had* been blood.) And suddenly, it made sense to me that he worked in a blood bank. The fear of garlic, no reflection in our mirror—that was our babysitter all over.

Finally, I closed the book I was reading and stared over at Jack in despair. "This is awful," I said. "Trevor and I are in trouble!"

I was half hoping Jack would tell me I was just

imagining things—but of course he didn't. He only nodded.

"Big trouble," he agreed solemnly. He pointed to the dusty old book *he*'d been reading. "It says here that vampires attack when people go to sleep. That's probably why Vincent wants you guys to go to bed early—so he can be sure you're sleeping when he comes upstairs to drink your blood."

"But why does he *want* our blood?" I wailed. "He works at a blood bank! Isn't that enough for him?"

"Probably not," said Jack. "Vampires are supposed to have insatiable thirsts. Anyway, Vincent would probably be fired from his job if too much blood disappeared. I bet he just sneaks a little once in a while to keep himself going. For a real meal, he needs the blood from a whole person."

And what better prey than two helpless kids alone in a deserted beach house?

"He'd better keep out of Trevor's room, then," I said. "My brother will wake up if a pine needle falls off a tree outside. Hey, maybe that's a good thing! If Vincent tries to go in there, Trevor will wake up and scare him off. Oh, I forgot. Vincent knows what a light sleeper Trevor is. I bet he just leaves him alone."

"Probably so. He'll probably try your room,"

suggested Jack comfortingly. "Does he babysit a lot at night?"

"Yes! Like three or four nights a week! In fact, he's coming *tomorrow* night! What am I supposed to do?" I could feel my voice starting to get raggedy. "Never go to *sleep* again?"

"Um, no. I'm sure that wouldn't . . ." Jack was leafing absently through his book while he talked. "Hey, wait a minute!" he suddenly said. "I just found something!"

I blew my nose. "What is it?"

"It's what we have to do to get rid of Vincent! Listen, here's the spell we have to say!"

He began to read out loud excitedly.

"*I conjure and command thee, spirit of the deceased, to answer my demands. Berald, Balbin, Gab, Gabor, Arise, Arise, I charge and command thee.*"

Jack looked up at me in triumph.

"What are you talking about?" I asked blankly.

"It's a spell to get rid of vampires! It's right here in this book!"

I didn't know what to say.

"Are Arise and Arise names, too?" I finally asked.

"I don't know. I don't think so," Jack said.

"Who are Berald and all those guys, anyway?"

"I don't *know*," said Jack irritably. "The point

is, we can use this spell to get rid of Vincent! All we have to do is say it over his grave, and—"

"His *grave!*" It came out in a little shriek. From across the room Mr. Stives raised an eyebrow at me. "What grave?" I said more quietly. "Vincent's not dead!"

"Yes, he is. He's undead, anyway."

"*Un*dead? So he's alive! He doesn't *have* a coffin! That's just what I was saying!"

Jack sighed. "It's really too bad you've never watched horror movies, Meg. It would save me a lot of time explaining. Anyway, here's the way vampires work.

"Vincent died once, see. And was buried. Then he came to life again, as a vampire."

"Why?"

Jack frowned at me for interrupting him again, but it seemed like a perfectly reasonable question to me.

"Well, why did he come back as a vampire? When my grandfather died, *he* didn't turn into a vampire!"

"Oh. I see what you mean. Actually, your grandfather might have, because there are lots of ways that you can turn into a vampire. If a vampire drinks your blood—if, say, Vincent sneaks into your room and drinks *your* blood some night," Jack added helpfully, "then you'll become a vampire yourself. Or if you die after someone has cursed you, you can turn into one, too."

Instantly, I decided that I would never give anyone any reason to curse me.

"This book has some other ways, too," Jack continued. "Like if you're the seventh child in your family, you're pretty sure to turn into a vampire. Or if you tell a lie in court—but I bet that one doesn't work nowadays. Anyway, Vincent came back to life as a vampire. Now he comes up out of his grave every night and wanders around looking for other victims."

"And then he goes back to his grave?" I asked.

"Yup. Always. Vampires sleep in their coffins. They can't be out in the sunlight—it would destroy them. So they always have to return to their coffins before dawn. And they have to sleep in the dirt they were buried in. If you move their graves, they have to move, too."

"Wait. I don't get that, either. I saw Vincent carrying his coffin down on the dock." (Now I knew that that really *was* what he'd been carrying.) "That was during the day! And he has to work during the day, too!"

Jack paused, glaring at me. I could tell he didn't like my mentioning anything that might wreck his theory.

"Was the sun actually *shining* when you saw him carrying his coffin?" he asked accusingly.

"No," I said. "Come to think of it, it was really foggy that day. And I think it's been foggy or rainy every time he's had to sit for us during the day."

"No problem, then," said Jack triumphantly. "Vincent can probably walk around in the fog without any trouble. And the medical center is surrounded by woods, so he can get inside the building without having to be out of the shade for more than a second."

"But, Jack, how could he be sleeping in the dirt he was buried in? If he did carry his coffin over on the ferry, he must have been buried somewhere on the mainland, don't you think?"

Jack paused. "Good point. Maybe he carries the dirt around inside his coffin. That might work."

Having solved the problem, he rushed back to the stuff that really interested him. "Anyway, we've got to *find* the coffin before we can do anything to him."

Suddenly, I remembered how Vincent had lurched off into the woods the other night. He had been heading in the direction of that deserted hunter's shack. That would be a perfect place to store a coffin. I mentioned it to Jack.

"I bet you're right," he said enthusiastically. "This is neat, Meg! We're vampire detectives!"

I wouldn't call it that neat. First of all, vampire detection isn't exactly the career I'd dreamed about. And second, it seemed to me that an awful lot of our "detective" work was just Jack imagining the way things *might* be. But everything he was saying did make a horrible kind of sense. I hated to admit it, but I was pretty sure he was right.

"And the book I've got here tells what we're supposed to do to get rid of Vincent when we do find him in his coffin," Jack went on. "*Now* do you get it?"

"I—I think so."

"Good. Of course we have to prepare first. We have to wear used graveclothes and eat dog meat and unsalted bread for nine days."

"*Dog meat!*" I gasped. "No *way!*"

The little boy who had wanted the Spiderman stuff looked over at me with interest.

"That's what it says in this book," Jack said.

"No dog meat," I said firmly. "Come on, Jack! What would Trucker say?" Trucker is Jack's basset hound.

"Oh, okay," said Jack. He seemed to be secretly relieved. "But we do have to drink grape juice—*that* part won't be so bad, anyway. Then on the ninth day at midnight, we draw a circle around the grave and make a bonfire out of herbs and stuff."

"What do you mean, 'stuff'?" I wasn't sure I really wanted to know.

"Oh, henbane," Jack told me offhandedly, "and aloes and mandrake. Stuff like that. Then we open up the grave and repeat that spell I just read to you."

"And then Vincent's out of the way?"

"Uh, not quite," Jack admitted. "We have to drive a stake through his heart first. But I can do that part if you don't feel like it."

Now I was staring at Jack in total shock.

"Hey, it will get rid of him! Isn't that what we want?" Jack asked.

"We have to wear graveclothes—whatever horrible things they are—and find *henbane* and dig open a *grave* and drive a *stake* through his *heart*—just to get rid of Vincent?" I asked furiously. "That's not fair! Why can't we just call an exterminator?"

Jack was leafing through his book again. "We might not want to do the stake part," he said. "This part says it may work better if you cut off his head with a spade."

"If *I*—"

I broke off, shaking my head.

"If I cut—" Again I couldn't finish.

"All right! I'll do it for you!" said Jack impatiently. "But I should think you'd want to take a little responsibility. He's *your* vampire, after all."

"I don't care whose vampire he is! I'm not cutting off his head with a spade!" Then, suddenly, a new idea occurred to me. "Anyway, what if Vincent is just pretending to be a vampire? I mean, what if he's just a regular kid who wants people to *think* he's a vampire?"

"Oh, I'm sure he's not," Jack answered. He did seem to be a little worried, though.

"I know, but we don't have any proof that he's a real vampire. He could have looked all this stuff up in books, just the way we did. He might only be wearing makeup and weird clothes. And filing his teeth into points, the way my dad said. Maybe I didn't see him in the mirror because he was standing at the wrong angle or something."

"But the blood! You saw him drink blood, remember? And he didn't even know you were watching him!"

"I said I didn't *know* if it was blood," I reminded him. "I still don't. It could have been tomato juice. And maybe he likes keeping up his vampire act even when no one's watching."

I stopped then, expecting Jack to get all reasonable and prove why I was wrong. But he didn't. He just stared at me, looking a little pale. I could tell that he was really worried now. Once he starts working on a project, he hates to be distracted from it.

"I never thought of that," he admitted. "I

mean, I'm *sure* he's a vampire. No question. But since we can't prove it, I guess we should forget about the stake through the heart. And cutting off his head with a spade," he added with regret. "His family might sue, after all."

"Isn't there something else we could try before we even start looking for his coffin?" I suggested. "Some kind of—of vampire repellant or something?"

"A charm, you mean?" For the first time that afternoon Jack was treating me as though I had said something smart. "That's not a bad idea."

"Only let's not use that spell about Arise and Arise," I said. "It's too old-fashioned. It doesn't make any sense. And I'll never be able to say it without laughing. Let's make up something of our own."

So that was how we ended up checking out fifteen books about the supernatural and lugging them all the way to Jack's house. And by the end of the afternoon, we had come up with a pretty good collection of ways to ward off vampires.

I was feeling a lot better. I'd much rather wear cute little mustard seeds—they were in one of the charms we found—than eat dog meat.

As I was making a shopping list, I started to wonder about something. "Jack?" I asked.

"Yeah?" Jack was practicing a few stab-through-the-heart motions. I think he was secretly hoping he would need to use them after all.

"Remember when I said that Vincent might just be pretending to be a vampire?"

"Uh-huh." Jack lunged forward again with his imaginary stake held high.

"Well, how will we know if all these charms are working?"

Jack stopped in midstab. "Let me think this over," he said. "Oh, wait, I know what. If they ward him off, then we'll know he's a vampire. If they don't ward him off, then we'll know he's *not* a vampire—and then you won't have anything to worry about when he comes to babysit. So that'll be good! Right?" He finished triumphantly.

"But what if they ward him off because he's a regular kid *pretending* to be a vampire being warded off by charms?" I asked. It was a confusing sentence, but I was sure Jack knew what I meant. "Or, what if he's a real vampire, but the charms don't ward him off because they don't work?"

Jack and I stared at each other in dismay. Suddenly Jack's face brightened.

"Then we move on to the next step," he said cheerfully. "The stake through the heart! You should always try to look on the bright side, Meg."

62

CHAPTER SIX

Did you know that nailing a sprig from a hawthorn bush to your front door will keep a vampire from coming inside?

Did you know that if you throw a handful of mustard seeds at a vampire's feet, he'll be so busy trying to count each seed that he won't chase you?

Did you know that if you crow like a rooster, a vampire has to return to his coffin?

Did you know that if you put some food into a bottle, a vampire will turn himself into a piece of straw so that he can get into the bottle, and then you can cork up the bottle and burn it?

Did you know that none of these tricks work?

I already had my doubts about putting the food into the bottle. "It sounds so stupid!" I complained to Jack as we prepared frantically for Vincent's arrival.

"It isn't stupid. It's an old Bulgarian charm," Jack snapped. "If you don't want to try it, don't.

I just happen to think that we should try everything we can."

It was the day after Jack and I had taken all the vampire books out of the library. It was around ten to seven. Jack had supper at my house, but it wasn't a very fun meal. Both of us were getting edgy. At seven Vincent would be coming over, and we hadn't nearly finished getting ready for him.

I was sitting outside on the porch under the light—it was foggy and dark; no sun made it through the heavy cover. Frantically I was trying to memorize the routine we'd decided on. Jack, meanwhile, was hurriedly stuffing crumbled pieces of hamburger into the tiny neck of the only bottle we had been able to find—an old ink bottle. (I think he was extra-grumpy because he was hungry. He had stuffed half his hamburger from supper into his pocket to save for this charm. I didn't tell him, but it had left a big grease stain all over the back half of his pants.)

And both of us were trying to chew up as many raw garlic cloves as we could. If seeing garlic on TV made Vincent leave the room, maybe smelling it up close would make him leave Moose Island. Or that's what we hoped, anyway.

"So first we offer him the hamburger," I said

nervously, "and wait to see whether he turns himself into a piece of straw." I popped another clove of garlic in my mouth. I was getting so it hardly made me shudder anymore. "What happens if he *does* turn himself into straw? Is that when we throw the mustard seeds at him?"

"No. No. We cork up the bottle and burn it," Jack said through clenched teeth. He was trying to force an extra-large chunk of meat into the bottle.

"How can you burn a *bottle*?" I asked. "Glass doesn't catch on fire!"

"It melts," said Jack shortly.

"Gross! We're going to *melt* Vincent? That's too cruel!" I protested.

Jack stopped poking meat into the ink bottle to stare at me for a minute. "Believe me, Meg, if Vincent turns himself into a piece of straw, you won't mind melting him. Let's wait and see if I can even *get* any more of this stupid hamburger into this stupid bottle before we starting worrying about whether it's too cruel."

Just then my mother poked her head out the front door. "Meg, I'm going up to change. If you'd like, we can drop Jack off when we— Good heavens, darling! You *reek* of garlic!"

She actually backed up a few steps.

"Are you *eating* those things?" she asked in astonishment, pointing to the pile of garlic cloves in my lap.

"Just a little snack, Mom," I said quickly. "You know—kind of like an after-dinner mint."

"And what's *this*?" Mom pointed at the sprig of maple leaves I had tacked to the door. The book said you had to use hawthorn, but I hadn't been able to find any.

"Oh, just a nice summer decoration," I said vaguely. "I saw one like it in a book. Isn't it pretty?"

Mom eyed me in silence for a second. "I don't have time to wonder what's going on. We'll see you in a few minutes," she said at last and disappeared back into the house.

"That's a relief," I muttered to Jack. "Maybe she'll forget all about—"

"He's coming," Jack interrupted me. His voice was tense. "Look, see him? On the path."

I peered through the blanket of gray and finally made out Vincent striding toward us.

"Oh, no!" I whispered. "I'm not ready! I haven't rehearsed enough!"

"Great," Jack muttered sarcastically. "Want me to ask him to come back when you've had more time to practice?"

I didn't answer. Vincent was on our front lawn.

"Hi, Vincent," I called nervously. Then, before I could stop myself, I blurted out, "We're just sitting here. We're not planning anything."

Jack kicked my ankle. Hastily, I tried to fix things. "We're not scheming or anything or—"

Jack's kick was much harder that time. "Ow!" I couldn't help yelping.

"Good evening," Vincent said, eyeing me curiously. "*What* are you not scheming, exactly?"

"Oh, nothing. I-I'd like you to meet my friend Jack," I answered. "Jack, here's Vincent."

Jack shouldn't have kicked me, because he didn't do any better than I had. If Vincent hadn't sensed that something was up from the stupid way *I* was acting, Jack certainly gave him a clue.

"Hi, Vincent," he said with a smile. "Want some of this food in a bottle? It's really great."

"Food in a . . ." Vincent's voice trailed off. He took a polite step forward—and then, like my mother, he reeled backward. He yanked a handkerchief out of his pocket and crammed it up against his face.

"I cannot *bear* that garlic," he said in a stifled voice.

"Oh, really?" I asked innocently. "Are you sure you don't want to try some?"

"Cock-a-doodle doo! Cock-a-doodle doo!" came Jack's cry before Vincent could say a word.

"Not *yet*!" I whispered, but it was too late.

My parents reached the front door just in time to see Jack leap up, flap his arms like wings, and start crowing.

They stopped in their tracks and stared at him in amazement.

So did Vincent. He *certainly* didn't return to his coffin the way he was supposed to. So much for the rooster!

"Enjoying yourself, Jack?" asked Dad dryly. Then he, too, reeled back. "Wow, you guys really *stink*! What's the problem?"

"They're doing a garlic experiment," my mother said equally dryly. "I think we may have to tie you to the top of the car when we take you home, Jack. Otherwise you might poison us. We'd better take you now, by the way. I've got to be at the medical center by seven-thirty sharp." She and my dad started walking toward the car.

"Uh, okay, Mrs. Swain. Just a sec."

Jack grabbed my arm. "What about the mustard seeds?" he hissed at me.

"Oh! I forgot all about them!" I darted a glance at Vincent. He was still standing a few feet away from us, his handkerchief pressed against his face.

"I can't do it now!" I whispered. "Not with Mom and Dad watching! They already think we're crazy!"

"Oh, go on," Jack whispered back. "Maybe they won't be able to see through the fog. You've got to let me know if it works!"

"Jack, we really have to take you home now!" my mother called from the front seat of the car. "Come on, dear!"

Quickly, I pulled the tin of mustard seeds out of my pocket, flipped the lid off, and hurled it straight at Vincent.

For once in my life, I aimed right. The tin hit Vincent right in the forehead and bounced to the ground. A shower of tiny yellow mustard seeds sprayed into the air and fell into the grass.

And the one time in my life that I aimed right, it made no difference.

Vincent didn't start counting the seeds. He didn't do anything except rub his forehead and stare at me. So much for the mustard seeds!

But my mother had a fit.

"Margaret Swain!" she shouted, leaping out of the car and marching toward me. "What a rude way to treat Vincent! You apologize at once!"

"I-I'm sorry, Vincent," I said faintly.

"It does not matter in the least," said Vincent

from behind his handkerchief. He gave my mother the best bow he could manage under the circumstances. "Children must have their frolics."

Of course, Mom noticed his charming manners, not his totally alien way of talking. "*I'm* sorry, too," she told Vincent. "I don't know what's gotten into Meg tonight, but obviously I haven't brought her up right. I hope you'll forgive me." She turned and spoke crossly to Jack. "Hop into the car. And please try to exhale out the window."

I walked slowly back to the house and went inside, Vincent following. He stayed about ten feet behind me, but he walked through the front door without any trouble. So much for the sprig of maple leaves on the door!

If it had been a sprig of hawthorn, maybe it would have worked. If Jack had crowed more realistically, maybe that would have worked, too.

If we had rehearsed longer, all the charms *might* have worked. But the only one that had even *sort* of worked was the garlic. And fifty cloves of garlic would drive anyone away—not just a vampire.

I brushed my teeth for fifteen minutes before I went to bed.

A rush of air on my face woke me. A tiny breeze blowing on my cheek from—

I sat bolt upright in bed. There was something in my room. I could feel it moving.

And I could *hear* it flapping. It was flying crazily above me. Now it was swooping low over my head, now darting to the other end of my room, now swooping over my head again. It was circling my room, its wings beating wildly. Every time it came toward me, it moved a little closer to my face.

At first I thought it was a moth—which would have been bad enough—but then I realized that it was much, much bigger than a moth.

I wanted to scream. I wanted to scream so badly! But I was afraid I would scare my brother.

I was so frightened I could hardly breathe. But I tried not to be a coward—I really did.

It's just a bat, I told myself sternly. *Bats get into houses lots of times. They're good for the ecosystem, anyway. It will probably fly out the window in a couple of seconds. Now go back to sleep.*

I forced myself to lie down again. *Stay calm,* I ordered myself. *Think about Trevor.* Trembling, I squeezed my eyes shut.

Sure. It's *really* likely that anyone can get back to sleep with a bat swooshing around her head! I couldn't have been lying there for more than ten seconds before I realized that sleep was out of the question. I would have to get the bat out of my

71

room and back out into the ecosystem where it belonged.

Oh, where were my parents? Doesn't getting rid of bats come under the heading of things— like cleaning up throw-up—that kids can't possibly be expected to do for themselves? Once, long before, a snake had gotten loose in our living room, and my father had bravely trapped it in a shopping bag. Why wasn't he here to help me now?

Trembling, I sat up in bed. Across the room I could see that the window was wide open. Maybe I could kind of usher the bat toward it. . . .

The bat did another loop over my head and careened crazily to the far end of the room. While it was there, I leaned down quickly, scrabbled around under my bed, and picked up my tennis racket. The next time the bat flapped toward me, I was ready.

Trembling, I waved the racket rapidly through the air in front of me. "G-get out, get out! Go catch bugs *outside*!" I whispered through chattering teeth, as though ordering a bat to leave would really have an effect.

The bat seemed to get the hint, though. It hovered in midair, somewhat hesitantly, then swooped back to the far end of the room and out the window.

In less than a second, I vaulted across the room, slammed the window shut, and vaulted back into bed. I didn't even feel my feet touch the floor. I dove under the covers and pulled the pillow over my head. Even though the bat was gone, I wanted some *armor*.

You did it, I told myself proudly—when I was able to breathe again. *Congratulations.* Suddenly, I was very, very tired.

I must have fallen asleep under the covers, but of course no one can keep a pillow over her head for very long. When I woke up again, my face was out in the open as usual. And once again, I could feel a tiny breeze.

Before I was completely awake, something glided almost silently toward me and landed on my pillow. I heard the tiniest rustling against my shoulder.

The next second, two teeth pierced my neck.

That time I couldn't hold back the scream.

"HELP ME! HELP ME! SOMEONE PLEASE, PLEASE HELP ME!"

I still don't know how I did it. One second, I was in my room. The next, I was down the stairs in the living room.

And there—oh, thank heaven!—were Mom and Dad just coming in the door.

Upstairs, Trevor burst into his own set of screams.

I hurled myself at my parents. "Oh, Mom! Dad!" I sobbed. "There was a vampire bat in my room! It bit me on the neck!"

"*What?*" asked my mother, amazed. "You'd better go check on Trevor," she told my father over her shoulder.

"But, Mom, it's true!" Upset as I was, I still didn't bother mentioning that Vincent was the vampire. No way would my mother ever believe *that* was true.

"Honey, you had a bad dream," said my mother tenderly as Dad ran upstairs. "It was probably just a mosquito. Look, there's Vincent standing right behind you. He would never let a bat into the house!" She sounded as though she thought *I* was the six-year-old, not Trevor.

I turned to see Vincent smiling tolerantly at me. "How violent are the nightmares of today's youth," he said with a chuckle.

"It wasn't a nightmare!" I shouted at him. "You just shut up, Vincent!" I couldn't *stand* the smug way he was looking at me. I was sure he was thinking, "You'll never pin this on me, Meg." And it drove me crazy to think that he might be right.

"Oh, Meg." My mother hugged me. Upstairs, Trevor's screams were starting to die down. "It's hard on you having Daddy and me away so much, isn't it? Of course it makes you nervous."

Again came Vincent's maddening little chuckle. "Or perhaps it is the junk food she eats. All that pizza before bed disturbs your sleeping patterns, Meg."

He turned to my mother. "In any case, there are no vampire bats in the northeastern United States," he said.

Now, don't you think that was a weird thing to say? I certainly do. I mean, what *normal* babysitter knows about vampire bats? But my mother believed Vincent, not me. In the end, she sent me back upstairs with a pat on the head and a Kleenex in my hand.

"She must be going through a growth spurt," I heard my mother telling Vincent doubtfully, as I walked into my room. "She hasn't been herself all day."

I closed the door and turned on the light in my room.

"Are you sure you don't want a ride, Vincent?" asked my father, who had just gone back downstairs.

I walked slowly over to the mirror.

"Okay. Thanks again, then," said my mother. "See you soon."

I pulled back the neckline of my nightshirt.

I hadn't been imagining things. There on my neck were two puncture marks.

76

CHAPTER SEVEN

The second I woke up the next morning I leaped out of bed and ran to the mirror.

The puncture marks had vanished.

I know it sounds crazy, but I was disappointed. Have you ever felt really sick, and then been disappointed to find out that you don't have a fever? If you don't feel well, you at least want something to show for it.

And if you *know* you've been bitten by a vampire, you at least want to see the proof.

Besides, without the bite marks, I didn't have anything to show my parents. Not that they would have believed me anyway. I could imagine how the conversation would have gone. Mom and Dad would have said the marks were just mosquito bites, and I would have gotten angry, and then they would have gotten angry at *me* for not sticking to our bargain.

Our bargain! I smiled sardonically at myself in the mirror. (Or at least as sardonically as I could.

I don't exactly know what a sardonic smile looks like.) Was it really fair that I couldn't complain about a *vampire* babysitter?

At least the attack on my neck had proved one thing. Vincent definitely wasn't *pretending* to be a vampire.

I put on my clothes and went down to breakfast. In the kitchen Mom was on the phone.

"Hi, Vincent? It's Carla Swain."

I froze in the doorway. Not *again*!

"Tom and I will both be working late tomorrow night, and I was wondering if— Oh. Oh, of course. No, of *course* you should go. We'll try you another time. Have fun!"

Mom hung up the phone. "That's too bad," she said with a sigh. "Vincent can't babysit tomorrow night. He's going to a dance."

"Vincent? A *dance*?"

"Yup." Mom sipped her coffee discontentedly. "He says there's a dance at the community center, and he really wants to go. So what could I say? A boy's got to have fun with his friends once in a while."

I was absolutely sure that Vincent had no friends.

"But I bet that means that all the kids on the island will be there," Mom went on. "I won't be able to find anyone to sit. Oh, well. The medical center can do without me. Maybe there won't *be* any emergencies tomorrow night. Anyway, what would you like for breakfast?"

All I wanted was a piece of toast. But I ate it as slowly as I could. I wanted to stay in the kitchen until Mom left.

Finally she did leave, and I rushed over to the phone.

Jack's mother answered. "Hi, Mrs. Cornell," I said. "It's Meg Swain. May I please speak to Jack?"

"Meg, Jack's eating his breakfast now. Can I have him call you back?"

"This will only take a second," I persisted. I didn't want to pester Mrs. Cornell, but I had to make my plans right away.

Jack came to the phone still chewing something. "Hello, Meg," he said thickly.

"Hi, Jack! If our parents say it's okay, do you want to go to a dance tomorrow night?"

Suddenly it sounded as though Jack was spitting his breakfast all over the floor.

"A dance?" he sputtered. "No, of course I don't!"

I was horrified. "Oh, I'm not asking you to *go* to a dance! Don't worry!" I lowered my voice and quickly filled him in on what had happened the night before.

"You don't think *I'll* turn into a vampire, do you?" I asked nervously.

"No, not if he only bit you. They have to drink your blood for it to work, I think. I don't think it works the first time around anyway—they have to bite you a few times. But what does this all have to do with the dance?"

"Oh, didn't I mention that? Vincent's going to be there. He just told my mother. I think we should try to follow him home and find out where he keeps his coffin!"

"Well, that's a relief," Jack said. "For a second I thought I was going to have to start ducking out of sight whenever you came by. Sure, I'll go to the dance. But, Meg, I have to warn you about one thing. I'm not putting *one toe* on that dance floor. I'm not even letting my *breath* touch that dance floor. So don't get any ideas."

"Dream on," I said scornfully.

Have you ever seen a vampire dance? No, you probably haven't. If you ever had, you would have remembered it.

Vincent really stood out in the crowd. And not only because he was about a foot taller than everyone else in the room and so pale that he practically glowed in the dark. It was more his— his dance techniques that were making him stand out. He was lurching around the crowded dance floor as if someone were yanking him around on a rope. Or as if he were a wind-up toy that someone had wound up much too tightly.

Even so, he had plenty of people to dance with. There were about five hundred times more girls than boys at the dance.

Moose Island must have just about as many boys as girls, but you'd never guess it from our community center. All kinds of stuff goes on there, from nature walks to concerts to sailing classes to ceramics classes to a horrible, disgusting poetry-writing workshop for kids that my mother made me go to the summer before because the man teaching it was a friend of Dad's. (We had to *act out* our poems.) And at every single event, there were never more than three or four boys.

So all the girls at the dance put up with Vincent's stylistics, as Jack called them.

After a few minutes he also called them boring. "This isn't getting us anywhere," he shouted into my ear. "We can't just stand around all night long watching Vincent dance!"

"Maybe we could hear what he's talking about if we went out and kind of danced next to him," I blared back.

"Uh-uh. No way. Anyway, we *wouldn't* be able

to hear anything. I can't even hear anything right now!"

"Jack, you sound like my mother complaining about MTV! What kind of spy are you? We can lip-read!"

"Forget it, Meg!" Jack shouted back. "I'm *not going out* on that dance floor! That's our deal. I don't have to dance, and you don't have to eat—

"DOG MEAT," he suddenly bellowed into a silent room. The song had just ended. And the lights came back on at the same time, so everyone around us got to take a nice, long look at Jack. It was quite mortifying.

I was relieved to see that Vincent hadn't turned around, though. He was having a talk with some girl. I couldn't see her face, but she was nodding in a very exaggerated, very stupid-looking way. "I *really, really, really* agree with you," her nod was saying.

"We're going to take a little break now," the guitar player announced. "Don't go away!"

Jack was scarlet-faced. "I *am* going away," he muttered. "I can't believe everyone turned around to stare at me. They probably think I *wanted* to be here!"

"No, wait a minute, Jack!" I whispered. "Look over there! Vincent's going out the back door with that girl!"

"So what?" Jack muttered. "If you think I'm

going to spy on some big lovefest, you're really out of your mind!"

"But, Jack, that girl's in trouble! She's out there alone with him!"

"I'm sure they had health classes in her school," Jack said grumpily. "She can take care of herself."

"Jack, I'm not talking about *that*! I'm saying that she's out there alone with a *vampire*!"

"Oh. I see what you mean. Hey, wait a minute! We've got to get out there and rescue her!"

"Exactly," I started to say, but Jack was already pushing his way toward the back door.

I followed along as fast as I dared. I hate even having to pass older kids on the sidewalk, let alone shove my way through a big mob of them. But finally, I made it to the back door, and only one kid spilled soda on me.

Jack was standing on the back steps, staring intently into the darkness. "He took her into those trees back there," he whispered, and pointed at a thin strip of woods behind the parking lot. "Let's go!"

I think Jack made a bigger deal of sneaking across the parking lot than he really had to. I mean, it was *dark* out there. There was no reason why we had to inch across all that asphalt on our stomachs!

"This is like crawling on sandpaper!" I whispered furiously at one point. "I bet I don't have a bit of skin left on my knees or elbows!"

"Well, we have to do it *right*," Jack whispered back. "In movies, they always crawl toward the enemy on their stomachs."

But that's through the jungle, not a parking lot! By the time we reached the edge of the woods, my elbows were rubbed raw. And I didn't even want to think what my clothes looked like.

When I saw Vincent and his friend, though, I forgot all about my clothes. The two of them were standing under a tree about ten feet away, their backs to us. Jack grabbed my arm and pointed to another tree, a huge one, that was right on the edge of the parking lot. The two of us tiptoed toward it (Jack in a much more secretive way than was really necessary). When we were safely behind the tree, we peeked out cautiously at Vincent and the girl.

I had to bite back a yelp of surprise. The girl Vincent was with was Melissa Gittes, the cheese-cake-eating babysitter we had tried out before Vincent!

What if she was babysitting for some other kids now? What if Vincent turned her into a vampire? Then all the kids *she* was sitting for would be in danger, too! (Unless they had already starved to death from her eating all the food at *their* houses.)

And Vincent was bending over her right now—

"Ow!" Melissa cried. "What was that?" She jerked away from Vincent and slapped her neck.

Vincent straightened up quickly. "I—I believe it was merely a mosquito," he said. "You have some kind of bite there, in any case. That is what I was trying to see."

He raised his head. And I saw that in the moonlight, his teeth were gleaming red.

I couldn't help it that time. I let out a gasp. And of course, Vincent turned and saw me right away.

Now I knew what people meant when they talked about their blood running cold. Mine felt so cold I couldn't move.

But I couldn't move anyway. There was nowhere to go, now that Vincent had seen Jack and me. And too many people were in danger now for me to run away and pretend I hadn't seen anything.

We weren't going to be able to follow Vincent home that night. But at least we could protect the other kids at the dance.

I took a deep breath and stepped out from behind the tree. I was about to say something like, "Yes, Vincent. We know everything about you now." But I guess that some part of my brain was still working.

"Hey, guys!" I said instead. "Hi! Wasn't it great

of Mom and Dad to let me come to this dance with Jack?"

"Wait a minute," said Jack. "They didn't—"

"Oh, hi, Meg," interrupted Melissa with a flustered laugh. Vincent was glaring furiously at Jack and me. He didn't say anything at all.

"And Mom and Dad said we could stay here right until the end, too!" I prattled on. "We're having a really great time! Aren't we, Jack?"

"We—we sure are," said Jack gamely.

"But I'm really glad to see you guys. Because Jack and I don't know a lot of the other kids here. So now we can hang out with the two of you!"

"That would be very—" Melissa obviously couldn't think of any polite way to finish the sentence.

"Yes, it would, wouldn't it?" I said happily. "Hey, listen! There's the band starting up again! Let's go back and dance some more!"

"No," said Vincent firmly. "Melissa and I wish to sit this one out."

But Melissa gave a little shrug. "Actually, we might as well go back inside," she said. *Now that these dumb kids have spoiled our romantic mood*, I could tell she was thinking. "I'm getting hungry anyway."

"Hey, me, too!" I said. "Let's *all* go get something to eat! And then we can dance some more!"

I don't know who was more upset about this—Vincent or Jack. But for the next two hours, Jack and I never let Vincent out of our sight. Every time the band took a break, we planted ourselves right next to Vincent and whoever he was dancing with at the time. And when the dance was finally over and my parents came to pick us up, I saw Vincent storming away down the street. Alone.

We hadn't had a chance to find out where he lived. But at least we had kept him from drinking anyone's blood.

Now all we had to do was make sure he would never get the chance again.

CHAPTER EIGHT

"No more dances," said Jack firmly. "Not ever."

"Fine," I agreed. "Dances won't help us get rid of Vincent anyway."

It was the morning after the dance at the community center. "The most romantic evening of my life," I kept calling it, just to torture Jack. He and I were sitting out on his dock dangling our legs in the water (just for a few seconds at a time, since the water was like ice), poring through our vampire books, and trying to decide what our next anti-Vincent move would be.

"After all," I said, "Vincent's been foiled from drinking people's blood twice in the past three days. He must be getting hungry. Or thirsty, or whatever you call it. We've got to stop him before he bites anyone, Jack. Otherwise, there will be *two* vampires on Moose Island."

"Maybe more," Jack pointed out. "Once Vincent turns someone else into a vampire, that person can drink *other* people's blood and turn *them* into vampires." He patted his own neck thoughtfully. "We've got enough summer people on the island. We don't need summer vampires, too. I have to tell you, Meg, I don't see any way around using that stake through the heart." Actually, Jack sounded quite cheerful about the idea. "None of our charms worked. It's time to bring in the heavy artillery. Do you have any wooden stakes around?"

"Nope," I said firmly.

"Oh. Well, we could use a silver bullet," Jack suggested, leafing through the book on his lap. "This author seems to think that works pretty well."

I snorted. "What are we supposed to do—*spit* the bullet into Vincent? Even if we did have a bullet, we don't have a gun!"

"Oh. That's true. But this book also says you can tear out the vampire's heart and—"

"You keep trying to get too fancy, Jack," I said hastily. "Let's not tear *anything* out. No tearing, and no shooting. No violence at all."

"Okay, how do *you* want to finish Vincent off?" Jack asked indignantly. "Should we just politely ask him to leave?"

"There's got to be some kind of middle ground between doing that and tearing his heart out!" I paused for a moment, thinking. "Let's see. Vincent can't be out in the sunshine, right?"

Jack nodded.

"What *happens* to vampires if the sun shines on them?"

"I don't know exactly," Jack confessed. "Maybe they evaporate. But for whatever reason, they're supposed to be back in their coffins before the sun is up."

"Then what if we nailed Vincent's coffin shut before he could get back inside?" I suggested. "Then he'd evaporate—or whatever vampires do—and we'd be finished with him! Wouldn't that work?"

"I bet it would!" Jack was starting to look excited. "It's worth a try, anyway. It would be cool to watch a vampire evaporate."

"We could sneak out some night and get to his coffin before he does," I said. "Didn't you say that vampires spend the night looking for victims? If we snuck out at around midnight, we'd have a few hours before Vincent even thought about coming back to his coffin."

"I've always wanted an excuse to sneak out of my house at midnight," said Jack eagerly. "When do you want to try it? The next time Vincent babysits?"

"No. I can't leave Trevor home alone with

him. Even if Trevor *is* a light sleeper, it would be too dangerous. And what if Vincent came into my room and found out that I was gone? No, we'd better do it tonight. Mom and Dad are going to be home, and they'll probably go to bed early. They usually do, on the nights they don't have to work."

"Okay," Jack agreed. "I'll bring a hammer and nails with me. Now what else do we need?"

"Some more garlic, just to be on the safe side. And what about herbs and stuff? The books keep talking about them. Should we take some along to sprinkle around his coffin once we've nailed it shut?"

"Sure. They might weaken him—and the weaker, the better."

Of course all the herbs the books talked about were supposed to weaken Vincent while he was *in* the coffin, and our whole idea was to keep him *out* of his coffin. But I figured a little herb sprinkling couldn't hurt.

We knew we wouldn't be able to find mandrake. But hemlock, saffron, and wood would be easy. There were some nice big hemlock bushes in front of Jack's house, and we could buy saffron in the fancy section of the grocery store.

"What kind of wood does the book mean, though?" I asked. " 'Wood' seems so unspecific! Are they talking about a log or something?"

"You can't really sprinkle a *log* around a grave," Jack pointed out. "I'll bring some sawdust from my dad's workshop. That should work fine."

"Okay. I'll bring the spices."

We sounded as though we were planning a potluck supper. I half expected one of us to volunteer to bring potato salad.

When we finished deciding who would bring what, Jack and I made our plans for that night.

I was going to stay awake until after my parents had fallen asleep. Over at his house, Jack was going to stay awake, too. At midnight he would sneak over to my house and hide in the garage. My parents always park the car outside (in a one-car garage, there's never enough room for the car), so they wouldn't see him.

As soon as I came out to get him, Jack and I would sneak into the woods and find that deserted hunter's shack.

But what if Vincent's coffin wasn't there after all?

And if the coffin *was* there, what if Vincent arrived at the same time we did?

Or what if he decided to catch up on his sleep, instead of hunting for victims? What if, when we got there, he was already sleeping in his coffin? Were we supposed to dump him out onto the ground or something?

What with one worry and another, I was pretty sure I wouldn't have much trouble staying awake that night.

It was almost midnight, but unfortunately my parents were taking their time about going to bed. I could still hear them talking downstairs. I was sure Jack was getting impatient down in the garage. Why had Mom and Dad picked *this* night to stay up late? Why didn't they realize that they needed their sleep so I could sneak out?

I tiptoed across my chilly bedroom floor and peeked out the window. Unfortunately, there wasn't much of a moon that night. No matter what time I got outside, it was going to be very, very dark.

Jack was probably starting to wonder if I'd forgotten our plan. He might even be about to—

Suddenly I heard footsteps coming up the stairs. Not Vincent's creepy footsteps, though— just my parents' normal ones. I tiptoed back across the floor, jumped into bed, and pulled the sheet up around my face so they wouldn't notice that I was still dressed.

And just in time. The door opened a crack, and my father peeked in.

"Meggie? Are you awake?" he whispered.

I kept my breathing slow and even, just like

all those heroines in old-fashioned books who are about to sneak out of the house.

Dad gently closed the door again. "She's out like a light," I heard him whisper to my mother.

"I'll just check on Trevor," Mom whispered back.

"Who is it?" I could hear Trevor blaring out loudly.

"It's Mom, honey," my mother answered in a low voice. "You go on back to sleep now." After a minute I heard her padding down the hall to her and Dad's bedroom.

I closed my eyes and tried to beam a message down to Jack. *Don't worry! I'm on my way!*

But it was almost half an hour before I finally dared to tiptoe down the stairs and out to the garage. Pooch tried to follow me outside, but I shoved him back as I closed the door.

It was cold and damp outside. I was just wearing a skirt and a T-shirt. I shivered and rubbed my arms as I stared into the dark garage.

"Jack? Ready to go? I'm sorry it took me so long!"

There was no answer. Had Vincent found Jack out here and—

"Jack!" I whispered frantically. *"Jack!"*

"JACK!" I said out loud.

"Wha'?" came Jack's thick, drowsy voice. " 'Zat

you, Mom? I'm jus' . . ." The rest trailed off into a murmur.

Jack had fallen asleep!

"Oh, why can't you be more like Trevor?" I groaned.

I dashed over to him, absolutely boiling with rage. I couldn't turn on the light, of course. But now that my eyes had adjusted to the dark, I could see that Jack was curled up on a pile of burlap bags. I grabbed his shoulder and shook him as hard as I could.

"Jack! Jack! Get up!"

Jack lifted his head. "Why? It's not a school day, Meg," he said clearly. And his head dropped down again.

Well, if there's anything more maddening than trying to keep your best friend from *sleeping through* a vampire hunt, I don't know what it is. I finally had to poke Jack with a trowel to wake him up.

That did the trick, though. "Meg! Hi! We have to get going! Hi!" Jack garbled, jumping to his feet. "Is that you? Ready to go?"

"I've been ready for hours. How about you?" I asked loftily.

Jack rubbed his eyes. "I—I guess I dropped off. I don't know how—those bags aren't even comfortable."

"I guess it doesn't matter. Did you bring your stuff, at least?"

"It's right here."

"Okay, let's put everything in this." I held out a canvas bag that had been hanging on a nail in the wall, and Jack dropped his stuff in.

Then we peered out of the garage. The sliver of moon that had been out a half-hour earlier was covered by clouds now. Suddenly, the night seemed a hundred times darker.

"What are we going to do? Just wander around in the dark until we find the shack?" I asked.

"I don't think we have any choice," Jack answered.

He was right. I just hoped that we found the hut before Vincent found us.

"Help!" I shrieked in agony. "Oh, Jack, you've got to help me!"

Jack grabbed my arm in the dark. "What's the matter?"

"I just stepped on a slug or something! Oh, it feels all squishy under my foot!"

Jack dropped my arm. "Is that all?" he asked in disgust. "I thought there was something really the matter!"

"Sorry," I sniffled, scraping my shoe off the best I could. "I guess this is all starting to get to me."

Stumbling through the woods in the pitch-dark *does* start to get to you after awhile. And Jack and I had been doing it for more than two hours.

We were streaked with mud and covered with scrapes. We had gotten smashed in the face by dozens of tree branches and tripped too many times to count.

Worst of all, we had absolutely no idea where we were. We had followed what we thought was a trail to the hut for as far as we could before we realized that it wasn't leading anywhere.

Now it had been more than an hour since we walked on any kind of path at all. We were forcing our way through underbrush that had probably never been stepped on by humans before. We could have been miles from anywhere, or just down the road from my house. But I was starting to suspect that the first possibility was the right one.

Tears filled my eyes as I stumbled blindly along. I couldn't help it. I was too cold and tired to feel brave anymore. Even if Vincent didn't find us and kill us, Jack and I were going to die. We would starve to death out here, and our bodies would never be found. . . .

"I wish we had brought a flashlight," Jack said quietly in the darkness next to me. And I knew his thoughts were running in the same direction as mine.

"I wish we had brought some water," I said after another fifteen minutes.

"I wish we hadn't thought of this stupid idea," said Jack fifteen minutes after *that*. Once again our thoughts were running in exactly the same direction.

"I wish we had never been born."

I glanced at my watch, which has hands that glow in the dark. It was almost four A.M. "Let's just give up and try again another night. It'll start to get light pretty soon," I pointed out. "And we're probably going in circles anyw—"

Thump! Looking back at Jack, I had just smashed into something. Something hard, flat, and wall-shaped that knocked the wind right out of me.

"What was *that*? Are you all right, Meg?" asked Jack in a frightened voice.

"I—I think so," I gasped when I could breathe again. I was running my hands over whatever was in front of me.

Suddenly, I realized that I was touching a window without any glass in it. I moved my hands a little farther, and felt the outlines of a door.

Now I knew where we must be.

"Jack!" I said excitedly. "We're here! This is the hunter's shack!"

I could hear Jack stumbling toward me. "Hey, great!" He ran his hands over the little building,

100

too. "And even if this isn't where Vincent's been camping out, I know where we are! We can easily get home from—"

At that moment the sliver of the moon finally slid out from behind the clouds that had been hiding it for the past couple of hours. A thin, watery beam of light shone down through the window of the shack.

There was just enough light for us to see the coffin on the floor.

It was what I'd been expecting, but I think I screamed anyway. I know Jack let out a startled gasp.

This *was* Vincent's hideout.

Shaking, I leaned against the wall of the shack. Our search was over at last.

Jack was still peering through the window. "The coffin's empty," he murmured. "Let's go right in and nail it up. We don't have much time before dawn."

Now I stared through the window myself. The long, black coffin was the only piece of furniture—if a coffin counts as furniture—in the room.

It was the loneliest bed I had ever seen.

I squared my shoulders. "Right. Let's go," I said. "It's getting lighter by the second." I strode resolutely toward the front door of the shack.

Just as I was about to step inside, I heard a

rustling noise. No, it was a *crashing* noise. And it was coming closer.

Terrified, I stared off in the direction of the sound. I could just make out a tall, pale, shadowy figure tramping through the underbrush.

In a few more seconds Vincent would be upon us.

CHAPTER NINE

At exactly the same time—and without thinking about it at all—Jack and I ducked around to the back of the shack and threw ourselves down into the tall weeds under the window.

We lay there, our hearts pounding, listening to Vincent plow his way through the underbrush toward us.

Our plan was wrecked, but I didn't care about that. All kinds of other things were running through my head. The grass was prickly and cold, and some kind of sharp stick was pressing into my ankle. I didn't dare shift position, though. I wondered what would happen if Jack or I sneezed, the way movie characters always seem to do in tight spots. What if the stuff in our bag clinked? Was there any chance we'd be able to talk our way out of *this* one by pretending we'd dropped in for a visit? Was there any chance I'd get to go to the bathroom in the next couple of hours? ("You should have gone before you left the house, dear," I could imagine my mother saying.)

Now Vincent was walking toward the front door. Trembling, I pressed myself down even harder. The stick pricking my ankle made me want to cry out.

This is how a hunted animal feels, I thought.

Now Vincent was pushing his front door open. Suddenly, he stopped—and sniffed the air.

"Blood," he muttered thoughtfully. *"Fresh blood."*

This was it. We were going to die.

But after a few more seconds, Vincent walked into the building and closed the door behind him.

I was shaking with relief. Carefully—so, so very carefully—I raised myself up to peek into the window. Next to me, Jack was doing the same thing.

Yes, Vincent was climbing into his coffin. He lay down and raised himself up on one elbow to adjust his cape around him. Then, with a heavy sigh, he lay down. In the faint moonlight I could see his eyes staring glassily up at the ceiling. He reached up and pulled down the lid of his coffin. It closed with a dull thud.

Then there was silence. We waited a little longer, just to be safe. (*Just in case he suddenly decides he wants a drink of water*, I found myself thinking idiotically.) But the coffin lid didn't budge.

I turned to Jack. "What are we going to do?" I

whispered. "How are we going to get him out of there?"

"I don't think we should even try," Jack whispered back. "We'll just have to nail the coffin shut with him inside it. At least that will stop him for a while."

I don't think I need to tell you that that was the *last* thing I felt like doing. We were lucky enough that Vincent hadn't seen us. Surely we wouldn't be lucky enough—if lucky is the right word—to nail him into his coffin without his catching us. Shouldn't we just cut our losses and escape right now?

But if we did, who would stop Vincent?

I picked up the canvas bag with our stuff in it and tiptoed around to the front door of the shack. Jack was right next to me.

Slowly, slowly I pushed open the door. It squeaked in protest, but nothing happened.

Ahead of us lay the coffin, stark and black. My heart was beating so hard I thought it would choke me. But I tiptoed across the floor, reached into the canvas bag, and pulled out the hammer. Then I reached back into the bag for the nails.

All I could feel was sawdust. "Hey, where are the nails?" I whispered to Jack.

"You were supposed to bring the nails," he answered.

Astonished, I turned and stared at him. "You

said *you'd* bring them. 'I'll bring a hammer and nails,' you said. Remember? We were out on the dock?''

"No way!" Jack said in his normal (loud) voice. "Why should I have to bring everything? We were supposed to be dividing up the stuff!"

"I brought the herbs!" I said, also in my normal (almost as loud) voice. "And the bag! Maybe you were too *sleepy* to remember the nails," I added nastily.

The light was still too dim to see clearly, but I could tell by Jack's voice that he was furious.

"*Girls!*" he said. "I should have known you'd mess this up!"

Now I was madder than I had ever been. "*I* messed this up?" I shouted. "You're the one who fell asleep! *I* managed to stay awake just fine! If only you'd had a little self-control, we—"

And then Vincent sat up in his coffin.

For a heart-stopping moment, everything froze. Then, for the second time that night, I screamed. This time, so did Jack.

"I cannot sleep with all this arguing," said Vincent calmly. And with a roar of rage, he vaulted out of his coffin.

Jack and I were out of that shack before we knew we'd started running. But Vincent was right on our heels.

He no longer seemed even a little bit human. He was nothing but a monster now—a wordless, roaring *thing* desperate to tear us to pieces.

Jack and I had bolted outside in different directions. At the doorway Vincent hesitated for a second. Then he took off after Jack.

"I can fend him off, Meg!" Jack shouted. "You go get help!"

But I didn't. Instead, I ran back into the shack. I couldn't nail Vincent's coffin shut now. But I had just remembered something—something Jack had mentioned the very first day we realized that Vincent was a vampire.

"Vampires sleep in their coffins. And they have to sleep in the dirt they were buried in."

I had asked how that could be, since I had seen Vincent carrying his coffin on the dock. And Jack had answered, "Maybe he carried the dirt around inside his coffin."

Frantically I dumped out everything in the canvas bag we had brought with us. Then I reached into Vincent's coffin.

There was a quilted lining at the bottom. I yanked it up. Underneath it was a layer of dirt.

Jack had been right!

I turned the coffin up on its end. It was incredibly heavy, but I couldn't let myself think about that. I scooped the dirt into my canvas bag. It was horrible work. The dirt was so fine and powdery that it kept sifting through my fingers. A cloud of it billowed out onto the ground. Panting with frustration, I shoved it into the bag as best I could.

Outside, Jack screamed again.

I couldn't waste more time inside. Quickly, I picked up a head of garlic that had rolled across the floor and rushed out with it.

I was just in time to see Vincent bare his teeth to sink into Jack's neck.

"No!" I shouted. In desperation, I took a huge bite out of the garlic. (Raw garlic makes a terrible midnight snack, by the way.) Then I rushed up— the canvas bag clunking maddeningly against my ankles—and pushed the garlic into Vincent's face.

With a bellow of rage, he let go of Jack and reeled backward. I grabbed Jack by the shoulder and pulled him away. And we ran.

Ran for our lives. Ran harder than we had ever run before. Ran for all we were worth. It's easy to come up with ways to describe it now—but you'll never be able to understand what it felt like unless you've been running through thick woods trying to get away from from a monster like Vincent.

It was getting lighter by the second. That

meant it was easier and easier for us to see where we were going—but it also meant that it was easier and easier for Vincent to see us.

But if we could outrun him just until the sun came up . . .

I darted a look over my shoulder. Vincent had found the hammer that I dropped. He was holding it up threateningly as he raced along. Already he was gaining on us. He had longer legs—and the canvas bag full of dirt was slowing me down.

"Why don't you drop that stupid bag?" Jack gasped.

"Can't!" I gasped back. Twigs were slapping me in the face. "Gotta have it!"

"But we can come back for it *later*! Your mom won't even know it's gone!"

"Gotta have it," I repeated hoarsely. Then I wrenched the head of garlic in half and handed half of the cloves to Jack. "Bite these and throw them back at him!" I yelled. "It may slow him down!"

It did. I could hear Vincent's footsteps faltering behind us in the underbrush. But I knew I couldn't keep running much longer. I'd been awake for almost twenty-four hours, and I was about to collapse from exhaustion.

I was certain that Vincent could keep up his pace for as long as he wanted to.

"Where can we *go*?" Jack panted.

As if it were answering my question, the ferry

horn suddenly sounded. The five A.M. ferry must be pulling in!

"Jack, that's it!" I gasped. "We can get on the ferry!"

If we could only be sure of getting there ahead of Vincent.

But luck was with us now. The woods were beginning to thin out, and through the trees I could see the outlines of a little dirt road and a few sleeping houses. They looked ridiculously calm and peaceful.

"That's Storrow Street!" said Jack. "If we run down to the end and take a left, we'll be only a couple blocks from the ferry dock!"

Well, it certainly seemed easier to run with some hope ahead of us. I was almost happy as Jack and I thudded through someone's backyard and onto Storrow Street.

The last of my garlic was gone. So was Jack's. But surely Vincent wouldn't dare attack us out in the open like this. . . .

I glanced back over my shoulder. Yes. It looked as though he *would* dare. He was coming faster and faster. And the look on his face made me want to faint.

Oh, where was the sunrise? Why wasn't it hurrying up? Didn't it *know* it had a vampire to evaporate?

The ferry horn blared again. It sounded much

closer now. It also sounded much too far away to help us.

"That's the last horn!" Jack said with despair. "The boat's about to leave! We'll never make it, Meg!"

Secretly I was sure Jack was right. But we couldn't stop now. I said the only thing I could think of to get him moving faster.

"*Boys!* I should have *known* there was no point in taking you along!"

That did it. Jack redoubled his speed, and so did I. We burst down Hatchet Hill, took a left onto Bluebottle Lane, and sped onto Main Street.

Ahead of us we could see the ferry. The last sleepy passenger was just walking up the gangplank. Above the ocean, the sky was turning pink.

For a second we stopped, dismayed. "We're too late!" I wailed.

"Don't stop! We can jump onto the gangplank from the dock! I've done it before!" Jack shouted.

We raced down to the dock.

"*Jump!*" Jack shouted and grabbed my hand.

With a final burst of energy, we leaped off the dock.

We landed on the gangplank one second before it closed.

CHAPTER TEN

Jack and I clung to the rail of the ferry, gasping for breath. The gangplank lumbered up onto the boat, and the ferry attendant snapped the gate into place.

The boat began to pull away just as Vincent dashed up to the dock.

I'll never forget the look of agony that blazed out of his eyes when he realized that the ferry was leaving without him.

"The dirt!" he howled. "I've got to have the *dirt!*"

"Dirt? What's he talking about?" Jack asked, bewildered. But I couldn't answer.

I *wanted* Vincent out of the way. I never, never wanted to see him again. But at that moment I almost felt sorry for him.

With a shriek of torment, he hurled himself into the water.

The boat was picking up speed now. Vincent was floundering desperately along through the water, but he wasn't making any headway. His long black cape and heavy shoes were starting to drag him down.

"Hey, fella!" called out the ferry attendant, who was still standing nearby. "Next boat's in an hour, y'know! It's not that long to wait!"

Vincent didn't reply. He just kept grimly thrashing along.

The ferry attendant shook his head. "Some folks'll do anything to get back to the mainland," he said. "Well, I guess it's time for a cup of coffee. Pretty sunrise, isn't it?" He disappeared down a flight of stairs.

The gap between us and Vincent was widening so fast that it was getting hard to see him. In another instant the sun slipped up over the horizon, and then we couldn't see him at all.

I turned to face Jack and drew in a long breath. "I guess vampires aren't the greatest swimmers," I said. "Most people know you're supposed to take your *shoes* off before you jump into the water."

Jack grinned shakily. "We shouldn't start feeling too great yet, though," he said. "He may still be there waiting for us when we get back. If the thing about sunrise doesn't work, I mean."

"No, he won't," I said serenely.

Jack looked startled. "What are you talking about? How do you know?"

114

I pointed to the canvas bag I was holding.

"What's in that thing, anyway?" Jack asked.

I held it open so that he could see the dirt inside.

"Wow, Meg," Jack said sarcastically. "I'm certainly glad you went to all that trouble to bring some dirt along with us. If Vincent had caught us, I would have been even gladder."

"This isn't just any dirt," I told him.

Jack took another look. "It isn't?"

"Uh-uh. Remember how you told me that vampires have to sleep in the dirt they were buried in? That they always have to have it near them?"

"Yes, I remember that."

"And you said the dirt Vincent was buried in might be in his coffin," I went on. "And I checked, and it was!"

Jack just stared at me for a minute. Then he clapped me on the shoulder.

"Good work!" said Jack. "I never would have thought of that! But why did you take the bag with you? You don't want Vincent to follow you around, do you?"

"Now, *that*," I said, smiling broadly, "is a really stupid question. Of course I don't. And he's not going to."

I lifted the bag high over the side of the ferry and dumped the dirt into the water.

"Meg, you're brilliant," said Jack.

"Yes, I certainly am," I agreed. "I'm so brilliant that I'm even going to take this bag down to the bathroom and rinse it out. The plumbing on this boat empties into the ocean. So every single speck of Vincent's grave will end up where it belongs."

"Scattered to the waves," said Jack dramatically. "Since you're so brilliant," he added in his normal voice. "I hope you can come up with a way to solve one little problem."

"Anything you say." I was bursting with confidence.

"You can figure out what to say to the ticket collector when he comes around."

Neither of us had any money.

"When's Dad going to be done working?" Trevor asked me a few days later. We were sitting on the curb outside Dad's office reading books we had brought along with us. Mine was *Daisy Morris, School Sleuth*. (There was a whole Daisy Morris series at the Moose Island library.) Trevor's was *Tyrannosaurus: Friend or Foe?*

"Pretty soon," I assured him. "He just has to finish up one little scene, he said."

My mother had been quite upset when Vincent hadn't shown up for his next babysitting date.

"Vincent is a very responsible person," she fretted at supper that night. "He would never cancel on me without calling. Something must have happened to him!"

"It certainly must have," I agreed gravely.

"He wasn't at the center today, either—I checked," Mom went on. She turned to my father. "Do you think I should call the police?"

"I'd wait a day or two," Dad advised her. "Maybe he's just not feeling well."

"I'm sure he's not," I said.

Two more days passed—pleasant, cozy days. Trevor and I started a shell collection and made some invisible ink together. (Unfortunately, it turned visible when we spilled it on Mom's and Dad's bedspread.) Vincent didn't show up at our house or at work. Mom got so worried that she finally did call the police. And they found no trace of Vincent on the island at all.

"He must have decided to go back to the mainland for some reason," Mom said sadly. "I just wish he had called to let me know. I guess he's not as responsible as I thought."

Trevor looked up from a dinosaur he was coloring and spoke the same thought that was in my head. "So who's going to be our babysitter now?" he asked.

Mom sighed. "I have no idea, honey. It's kind of late in the summer to look for someone who can come regularly. Most of the kids who work as mothers' helpers have already found their jobs."

"Couldn't we come along to work with you and play in the waiting room?" I asked. "We promise not to get in anyone's way!"

"Yeah! I could bring my dinosaurs along with me and show them all the operations and stuff!" said Trevor excitedly.

"Well, I guess that's what we'll have to do until we find someone to replace Vincent," Mom said with a sigh. "Not that we'll *ever* find anyone who's as polite as Vincent."

Trevor and I didn't bother answering that.

So when Mom and Dad had to work late, we just started tagging along. There was a small playroom at the center that was hardly ever used. Of course, I'm obviously too old to get excited about playrooms, but Trevor had a great time. And there was always a cart full of kids' books that I could read. They made a nice change from the books at the library. Some of them had even been written in the past decade.

When we had to tag along with Dad, we usually brought books, too. Or we drew on his scrap paper. There's always tons of scrap paper in Dad's office, as long as you get there in time to remind him not to crumple it up.

One day Trevor and I were sitting on the curb

outside Dad's office. (Don't worry. It's a very quiet street. No cars.) It was too nice to sit inside, watching Dad get cranky. So we brought our books outside.

I was just about to start reading Trevor a long, long, boring, boring book about *Triceratops* when I heard someone speak my name.

I looked up, and coming down the sidewalk was Libby Levin!

"Libby!" I cried, jumping to my feet. Trevor rushed over to hug her.

"What are you *doing* here?" I asked. "I thought you were at horseback riding camp!"

"I *was*," Libby said ruefully, "until I fell off."

She held out her left arm to show us. From knuckles to elbow, her arm was completely covered in plaster. "I broke it in three places," she said. "I'm not as good a rider as I thought."

"So what are you going to do for the rest of the summer?" I asked.

Libby shook her head. "I don't know. I guess I'll have to look for babysitting jobs. My mom told me you guys were already taken care of, though. Too bad. You would have been my first—"

"We're *not* taken care of!" Trevor and I both interrupted at the same time.

"Our babysitter's gone!" Trevor said happily.

120

Ann Hodgman

"And, anyway, he was the yuckiest person you ever saw in the *world*!"

"It's true," I told Libby with a smile. "He *was* the yuckiest person you ever saw in the world. But he—uh—he quit. And Mom and Dad haven't been able to find anyone to replace him. . . ."

And so Libby came back to babysit. Which is nice, because this will probably be her last summer with us. Mom and Dad have promised that *next* year, I'll be old enough to babysit, if I want to. So it will be *my* turn to terrorize the kids on Moose Island.

No, just kidding. I'll be really nice to them. Really, it's great the way everything has worked out. Libby is back, and Vincent is gone forever—in one way or another. Even if the sun didn't evaporate him, he can't possibly come back to Moose Island ever again. Not with the dirt from his coffin scattered to the waves.

At least not unless the tide washes the dirt back onto our beach. But, of course, that will never happen. I don't think so, anyway. I mean, I don't really see how it could.

It couldn't—could it?

ANN HODGMAN is a former children's book editor and the author of over 25 children's books, including the bestselling *There's a Batwing In My Lunchbox* and the Lunchroom series. In addition to humorous fiction for children, she has written teen mysteries and non-fiction for reluctant readers. She is also a writer for *The Big Picture,* a series of educational posters distributed in schools nationwide.

JOHN PIERARD is best known for his illustrations for *Isaac Asimov's Science Fiction Magazine, Distant Stars,* the bestselling *My Teacher Is An Alien* and several books in the Time Machine series. He lives in Manhattan.